# The Gallows at Graneros

**Center Point
Large Print**

**This Large Print Book carries the
Seal of Approval of N.A.V.H.**

# The Gallows at Graneros

## LEWIS B. PATTEN

CENTER POINT PUBLISHING
THORNDIKE, MAINE

This Center Point Large Print edition
is published in the year 2005 by arrangement with
Golden West Literary Agency.

Copyright © 1975 by Lewis B. Patten.

The text of this Large Print edition is unabridged. In other
aspects, this book may vary from the original edition. Printed in
Thailand. Set in 16-point Times New Roman type.

ISBN 1-58547-649-8

Library of Congress Cataloging-in-Publication Data

Patten, Lewis B.
   The gallows at Graneros / Lewis B. Patten.--Center Point large print ed.
   p. cm.
   ISBN 1-58547-649-8 (lib. bdg. : alk. paper)
   1. Large type books.  I. Title.

PS3566.A79G35 2005
813'.54--dc22

2005007730

# The Gallows
## at Graneros

# Chapter 1

In Spanish, the word *graneros* means "regions rich in grain," and while rich abundance might have been the dream of the first white settlers in this area, it had only been a dream. Graneros seldom got more than five inches of rain a year, which was not enough to raise anything but the scrub piñon and cedars that dotted the hillsides, and the sagebrush and the sparse grass that grew in its shade.

This country was cattle country and not exceptionally good for that. It took thirty acres of land to support each head of stock.

The town of Graneros sat on the bank of Conejos Creek, a stream that was dry 80 per cent of the time. The town got its water from the underground flow, tapped by more than a dozen wells.

The main street had the pretentious name of Graneros Avenue. The cross streets were identified by letters of the alphabet, A through K. First Street paralleled Graneros Avenue on the east. Second Street paralleled it on the west. And that was the town. Eighty-seven inhabitants. A sheriff because Graneros happened to be the county seat. A courthouse that looked like any other sand-blasted, false-fronted building along Graneros Avenue.

West, by twenty miles, was the boundary of the Apache Indian reservation. Now, in 1889, the Apaches were at peace. But it had been only three short years before that Geronimo had last been captured after another of his murderous forays. Nobody in Graneros had much confidence that the Apache scourge was a thing of the past, or that Geronimo would remain in custody. He had escaped before. But even if he did not, some other firebrand would emerge, take a handful of followers and their families and embark upon an equally savage trail of death.

With few exceptions, therefore, the people of Graneros hated Indians worse than a Baptist preacher hated sin. Most of them had lost friends or members of their families. They hoped that peace had come at last, even if they found it hard to believe. They prayed it might endure.

Down at the southern end of town where the old wooden bridge crossed Conejos Creek, there was a ramshackle wooden building that had been a stage station in the days before there was a town. It had fallen into disrepair. Its windows were broken and its door had long since disappeared, perhaps used by some transient for firewood. Cattle sometimes bedded down inside and the dirt floor was covered with several inches of dry manure.

Behind the shack were the remains of the corrals in which the spare stage horses had been kept. A windmill had drawn water from a well for the stage station and for the watering troughs inside the corral. Now, broken down and unusable, it slowly deteriorated in the sun, wind and infrequent rain.

What made this old stage station particularly notice-able was the gallows that had been built in front of it. In contrast to the windmill, it was still in good repair, having been constructed only two years before for the purpose of executing two killers the court had sentenced to death. It had been located here because material for it could be scrounged from the old stage station and corrals. There had been talk from time to time that it ought to be torn down but so far nobody had gotten around to it.

Thorpe Stedman was sheriff of Conejos County. On this September day he was serving an eviction notice for the Graneros Bank, a job he had very little stomach for. The man he served it on was Benny Fernandez but apparently Benny had been getting ready to pull out anyway because the eviction order didn't seem to upset him much. He even invited Stedman in and his fat wife gave the sheriff a cup of bad-tasting coffee brewed from roasted beans.

Stedman was a big, rawboned man, thirty-five years old. He had never been married but he was thinking about it now. The woman's name was Serena Van Vleet, a widow whose husband had been killed by Apaches a few years back when they attacked the stagecoach in which he was a passenger. Serena was a full-bodied, womanly woman with a warm smile and a pair of laughing eyes and a nice clean fragrance about her that made Thorpe Stedman want to get as close to her as possible. She supported herself by sewing and dressmaking, a livelihood Stedman knew was often desperately poor, but never had he heard her complain. She even gave money occasionally to her brother, which always irritated Stedman because he knew she needed it.

Thorpe Stedman got back to town at midnight. Something caught his eye as he rode past the old stage station and he stopped his horse for a better look. The horse, made suddenly nervous, danced and fought the reins. Stedman rode closer and what he saw made his belly turn to ice. A body was hanging from the gallows, swinging and turning ever so slightly in the breeze.

His horse wouldn't go any closer so Stedman dismounted and tied the animal to a clump of brush. He walked to the gallows.

There was no moon but there was a small amount of light coming from the stars. Enough to see the rope tied to the foot of one of the gallows supports. Stedman untied it and eased the body to the ground. Dark it was, but there could be no doubt who the dead man was. It was Billy Pinto, the simple-minded Apache Indian who lived a ways up Conejos Creek in a shack he had built himself, supporting himself by snaring rabbits and by sweeping out the Red Dog Saloon every morning before it opened up.

In a town like Graneros, where hatred of Indians was so strong, you wouldn't normally expect to find an Indian. The only reason Billy Pinto was tolerated was that he was as simple-minded as a child. Most people considered him harmless. Some distrusted him. But nobody liked him and nobody spoke to him. With one exception. That was Hughie Diggs, who folks said wasn't right in the head himself. Hughie Diggs and Billy Pinto were friends, drawn together perhaps by their similar affliction.

Squatting beside the body of Billy Pinto, Thorpe Stedman cursed softly beneath his breath. His first guess was that this was a simple act of hatred. Maybe some Apaches had broken away from the reservation and killed someone and this was the town's way of avenging it.

Finally he shrugged. He lifted Billy Pinto's body and carried it to his horse, surprised that the Indian was so light. He laid him face down across his saddle despite the horse's nervousness. Then, speaking soothingly to the horse, he led him across the bridge and up Graneros Avenue toward the jail.

It was hard to believe that Billy Pinto was dead. He had been so harmless, and it didn't seem possible anyone could have hated him sufficiently to do this to him.

Furthermore, several men had to have been involved. Now it was his job to find out who they were. An Indian Billy Pinto might have been. An Apache he also was. But he had been harmless and a human being and he had not been tried and found guilty of any crime. His death had to be accounted for.

Ben Hurd and his wife lived in a small, white-frame house on the southeast edge of town, hard against the bed of Conejos Creek. There was a small stable out in back of the house in which Ben kept his horse and a brown-and-white spotted milk cow.

The cow foraged in the bed of Conejos Creek, a bell hung around her neck. Usually she came home by herself around milking time. Some nights she did not and on those occasions, Susan, Hurd's sixteen-year-old daughter went after her.

Susan was a yellow-haired girl with blue eyes and a full-lipped, smiling mouth. At sixteen, she was fully developed, a fact that had not gone unnoticed in town. Susan was fully conscious of the attention paid her when she walked down Graneros Avenue and she relished it.

When Mrs. Hurd put supper on the table, Ben Hurd went to the back door and listened for the cowbell. He didn't hear it. He turned and caught a suddenly frightened expression on his wife's broad face. He said, "Pshaw. Nothing to worry about. The cow strayed farther than usual, that's all. I'll go after them."

But he picked up his rifle as he went out the door, knowing that doing so would further worry his wife but troubled himself, now, by vague uneasiness.

By now it was almost completely dark. He picked his way down the path through the cutbank to the flat bed of the creek. He headed downstream, away from town, the way the cow almost always went.

Now that he was away from the house he began to hurry. Most of the grass and weeds had long since been eaten off this close to the house so nothing impeded his progress. The creekbed was dry and sandy and what rocks were there were small.

Ben Hurd trotted half a mile, pausing often to listen for the bell. He was thoroughly scared and anxiously probing the shadows to right and left before he finally heard it faintly in the distance ahead.

Reassured, he slowed his pace to a walk. The sound of the bell grew louder, but not because the cow was approaching him. Moreover, the bell was not ringing the way it would be if the cow was being driven along toward home. The sounds came only intermittently, as if the cow was grazing, occasionally lifting its head to chew.

Hurd nearly called out for Susan. He changed his mind because of the unease that still troubled him. Gun gripped firmly in both hands, tense and now filled with fear for Susan's safety, he moved almost silently ahead.

The cowbell now was close. And suddenly, on his right, Ben heard another sound, that of Susan's voice.

He couldn't tell if it was a cry of fright, pain, or something else. His own fear told him it had to be a cry of pain. Whirling, his heart thumping hard in his chest, he plunged recklessly toward the sound.

There was a violent flurry of movement up ahead. A figure raised up, then plunged away into the dark. Hurd saw a spot of white where the figure had appeared from and yelled, "Susan! Are you all right?"

He'd had no time to fire at the disappearing figure and now all he was interested in was Susan's safety.

He knelt beside her. Because he knew what had been happening, the rage in him poured out like a flood. "Who was it? Tell me who it was!"

Thoroughly terrified, Susan was crying now. Crying not like a fully developed sixteen-year-old girl but like a child. And Ben Hurd did what he had done so many many times in the last sixteen years. He put his arms around her and let her cry out her fright against his chest.

And as he held her, his fury grew. Before Susan said a word, Ben's opinion of what had happened was already formed. The cow had strayed farther than usual. She might even have been driven purposely away so that Susan could be caught farther from the house.

Then the attacker had waited patiently for her to come. When she had, he had brutally attacked her. Had not Ben arrived when he had, she might very well have been killed to keep her from naming her attacker.

Gradually, Susan's wild weeping quieted, died to occasional, uncontrollable sobs. Ben gently stroked her hair. Finally, making his tightly furious voice as soft as possible he asked, "Who was it, honey? Who?"

There was an instant's silence, unbroken even by a sob. Ben repeated, "Who?"

Without answering, she began once more to weep. Ben waited again until her weeping had quieted. Then he persisted, his voice turning harsh, "Who? Who attacked you, honey? Damn it, you've got to tell me who!"

Again there was utter silence from the girl. Reluctantly the answer finally came. In a voice that was almost a whisper. "That Indian. Billy Pinto. He . . ." Again she began weeping hysterically but this time there was something about the weeping that seemed almost forced.

Raw fury, fueled by the fanatical hatred he already felt toward Indians, flooded through Ben Hurd's mind. He wanted to kill Billy Pinto with his hands.

But Susan was hurt, he still did not know how badly. His wife would be nearly frantic with worry about them both. He had to return. He had to take Susan home.

He lifted her in his arms. He got behind the cow and, carrying Susan, drove the cow toward home.

As he walked he thought that people in this town should have known better than to let a goddamned Apache Indian live in their midst. They should have known that something like this was bound to happen sooner or later.

But it wouldn't happen again. Ben Hurd meant to see that it did not. As soon as Susan was safely home in bed and being cared for by her mother, he meant to round up several men he could count on, men who felt the same way he did about Indians. They'd find Billy Pinto if it took all night. And by God he'd pay for defiling Susan the way he had. He'd pay. He'd pay.

Hurd was nearly running now, breathing hard both from exertion and from rage. The cow trotted ahead of him, bell clanging with every step she took.

Susan, inert in his arms, was utterly silent now. He thought she might be unconscious but he couldn't tell. Perhaps she had been hurt even worse than he had feared.

It never even occurred to him to doubt Susan's word.

## Chapter 2

The whole town was dark when Thorpe Stedman reached the jail. There was nothing he could do with the body of Billy Pinto but take it inside the jail. He tied his horse to the hitchrail out front, found his keys, and unlocked the door. He went in and lighted a lamp. Then he returned to his horse, eased the body off, and carried it inside. He laid it on the bunk in the corner, trying not to look at the Indian's face, which was blackish red, swollen, and completely unlike the way Billy Pinto's face had been in life. He covered the body with his blanket.

He was hungry, tired and irritable. There was no place he could get anything to eat at this hour of the night, so the hunger would have to wait. But he could have coffee. He crossed the room to the potbellied stove and opened the door. He stuffed some newspapers in, added wood, then lit the newspapers underneath. The stove began almost immediately to roar.

There was a bucket and dipper on a washstand in the corner opposite the cot. He half-filled the coffeepot, went to the door and after sloshing it around, dumped the old grounds and water into the street. Returning, he refilled it, added coffee, then put it on the stove.

He didn't suppose it was very nice of him to awaken Dallas Wagoner, but he was damned if he was going to spend the night here with Billy Pinto's corpse and he didn't want to spend the night away from the jail. He went out, carefully locking the door behind as if he suspected somebody would break in and steal the corpse. He smiled a little sourly to himself at the thought as he walked up Graneros Avenue to D Street and turned east toward First. Wagoner's house sat at the intersection of First and D. It had a picket fence with a squeaky gate. As soon as Stedman opened the gate, it squeaked and out back a dog began to bark.

Wagoner's front door had a twist bell. Stedman twisted it and when he got no response, twisted it several more times as hard as he could. A lamp was lighted in an upstairs bedroom and a woman's voice called out petulantly, "Who is it and what do you want?"

"It's Thorpe Stedman, Mrs. Wagoner. Tell your husband I've got a body down at the jail that needs taking care of."

"Can't it wait for morning?"

Irritation was on the increase in Stedman, and it showed in his voice. "No, ma'am, it can't wait. Tell Dallas to get on down to the jail right away."

She mumbled something that Stedman couldn't understand. The dog, apparently penned up in the

17

stable behind the house, continued barking. Stedman went down the walk and slammed through the gate. He returned to the jail, unlocked it, and went inside. Dallas Wagoner wasn't going to like being dragged out in the middle of the night to take care of the body of an Indian. But at the moment, Stedman didn't give a damn what anybody liked.

He got a cup and filled it with coffee, which had just begun to boil. He closed the damper on the stovepipe and the stove stopped roaring almost at once.

Scowling, Stedman sat down in the swivel chair behind his desk. It creaked as he did, reminding him of Wagoner's gate.

Why in the hell, he asked himself, would anybody hang Billy Pinto, who was just about as harmless as anybody could get? Hanging implied premeditation and a considerable amount of anger. It also implied the participation of several men, at least three, possibly a good many more. What could Billy Pinto have done anyway?

He stared gloomily at the blanket-covered corpse on the cot. He'd never thought much about Billy Pinto's age, but now he supposed the Indian had been thirty at least, even though he had seemed much younger. Thinking about it now, he realized that he had never even heard the Indian's voice. He had nodded, or spoken to Billy Pinto sometimes when he happened to pass him on the street, but the Indian had always replied only with a nod or a ducking of his head.

What else did he know about the Indian? Damned

18

little, he admitted with a touch of defensiveness. After all, it wasn't his job to pry into the private lives of the county's citizens. All he was supposed to do was serve papers and keep the peace.

Yet he knew that, by remaining ignorant of this strange and simple-minded Indian he had somehow failed to do his duty. His job should encompass more than the mechanical serving of papers, the apprehension of lawbreakers, and the jailing of drunks.

He wished Wagoner would come and get Billy Pinto's body out of here. But he knew it was going to take some time. Wagoner had to get up, dress, walk down to the livery stable and hitch a team to the hearse. Then he had to drive it here. It would take twenty or thirty minutes at least.

Billy Pinto's blanket-draped body continued to draw his glance. The Apaches must have driven Pinto out a long time ago, he thought. Indians had a superstitious distrust of those whose minds are different. Probably as soon as Billy Pinto had been old enough for them to tell he was different, they had driven him away. Which meant he'd probably spent most of his adult life in or near white settlements.

He finished his coffee and got another cup. He had no more than sat down with it when he heard horses' hoofs and the sounds of the hearse's wheels in the street outside.

He got up and went to the door. Dallas Wagoner came in, a bluff, overweight man with a florid face. He was dressed, even at this hour of the night, in a black business suit, a white shirt with a black necktie. He wore his black derby hat.

His glance went to the body on the cot and his face assumed what Stedman had always thought of as his "undertaker's expression." "Who is it, Sheriff?"

Stedman watched his face as he said, "Billy Pinto. He was hanged."

Wagoner tried to act surprised and he didn't do a bad job of it. But it didn't ring quite true as he said explosively, "Billy Pinto! That Indian? And you dragged me out of bed for him?"

Stedman said sourly, "He's a body, even if he can't pay for his own funeral. The county will take care of it so you don't need to get all upset."

Wagoner muttered something. He crossed the room and peeled the blanket back. Stedman had the feeling that at that moment he didn't want the sheriff to see his face. Stedman said, "You knew, didn't you? You knew that he was dead."

There was an instant before Wagoner turned, an instant when he stood frozen, absolutely motionless. When he did turn, his face showed an almost convincing surprise. "Knew? How the hell could I know?"

Stedman said, "All right. I'll help you carry him out." He crossed the room, took the blanket off Billy Pinto's body and laid it aside. He lifted the Indian's upper half and Wagoner took the feet. Ordinarily Wagoner would have brought a stretcher in, but there didn't seem to be any need for it tonight.

The door of the hearse was open. They laid Billy

Pinto's body in and Wagoner closed the door. He seemed to want to say something, and hesitated several moments. Finally he asked, "What about the funeral? Or will there even be a funeral? I never buried an Indian before."

Stedman said, "Let's think about that tomorrow."

"Sure. All right." Now, Wagoner seemed anxious to get away. He climbed to the seat, clucked at the team, and drove away up the dark and silent street.

Stedman stood watching for several moments. The hearse turned the corner and disappeared. Its sound died away. Thorpe Stedman suddenly felt like ringing the church bell and waking everyone in town. He wanted some answers and the truth was, he didn't feel much like waiting until morning for them. He resisted the impulse, and went back inside the jail.

He was tired, but he couldn't bring himself to lie on the couch where Billy Pinto's body had lain only a few moments before. He sat down in his swivel chair, finished his coffee, and rested his head on the back of the chair.

The puzzle haunted him. Why should they have hanged Billy Pinto who had never hurt anyone in his life, so far as Stedman knew? There could only be two possible answers to that. Either they had hanged Billy in blind reprisal for the act of some other Indian or Indians, or Billy had done something bad or they thought he had.

He closed his eyes. After a while he dozed. Half a dozen times during the night he snapped awake, then dozed off again. When light finally grayed the eastern sky, he got up, stretched, and built up the fire in the stove. He heated a pan of water first. Then, while he washed and shaved, he heated the coffee he had made last night. By the time he finished shaving, it was hot. He poured a cup and stood at the window sipping it, staring into the street.

He felt far from rested but his mind was beginning to absorb some of the complications that were going to result from Billy Pinto's death. The death of an Indian, particularly by violence, wasn't the same as the death of anyone else. Indians were under the jurisdiction of the Indian Bureau. The bureau had to be notified. When they knew the circumstances, they'd probably send in a U.S. marshal to investigate.

The hell of it was, Stedman didn't know where to begin his own investigation. Then he remembered Hughie Diggs. He and Billy Pinto had been inseparable. Maybe Hughie had seen something, or knew something about what had happened here last night.

He left the jail. His horse was still tied at the rail. He untied, mounted, and rode to the livery stable. He exchanged the horse for a fresh one and rode back out again.

The restaurant was just opening up. He dismounted and tied. He'd had no supper at all last night. It wouldn't hurt to take the time to eat something before beginning his hunt for Hughie Diggs.

Hughie Diggs was a long ways from town. He was

huddled under a cutbank in the bed of Conejos Creek, nearly five miles from the old stage station where Billy Pinto had been hanged.

All night he had huddled here, and now he didn't know what he should do next. He had been seen last night at the stage station after they had hanged Billy, his friend. He had fled, with one of them on horseback in pursuit. He'd lost the pursuer in the dark but he knew they'd be taking up the pursuit again today. He knew the face and name of every man who had helped hang Billy Pinto and they knew he knew.

Mingled with Hughie's fear was a strong sense of guilt. He should have helped Billy last night. He should have showed himself before they actually put the rope around Billy's neck.

He hadn't because he had been afraid. And confused. Besides, right up until the last moment, he'd thought it was only some cruel joke they were playing on the Indian. When he found out it was not, and rushed out, it was too late. Billy was swinging helplessly from the gallows, his feet well clear of the ground.

Two of the men tried to grab him. Before they could Hughie turned and ran. But, he thought now, if he'd run for help the minute they dragged Billy under the gallows, maybe it would have turned out differently. Maybe Billy would still be alive.

He crawled out of the hole in which he'd hidden himself. Fearfully he stared toward town. The early air was chill and Hughie shivered helplessly.

It terrified him to think of leaving Graneros. He hadn't the faintest idea where he could go. He had no food and not even a coat or sweater to keep him warm during the night.

Besides that, if he didn't show up for his job at the livery stable this morning, Mr. Lockman would probably fire him. He hadn't missed a day at work in the last five years. That was one of the reasons Mr. Lockman kept him on. He always showed up for work.

If he lost his job, he'd have to give up his room at the boardinghouse. He wouldn't have any money and that would mean he couldn't eat.

Miserably he started walking toward town. Fear made him stop. If he went back to town, they'd do the same thing to him that they had done to Billy. They'd hang him from that gallows in front of the old stage station. There'd been no reason for hanging Billy and there didn't need to be a reason for hanging him. But in his case there was a reason and a good one. He knew the men who had hanged Billy. He could tell the sheriff who they were. Maybe killing an Indian wasn't as serious as killing somebody white. But it wasn't something you could just do and not pay some kind of penalty.

No. There was really only one thing he could do. He had to run away. Being without food, or money, or any of his belongings was better than being dead, which was what he'd be if he tried going back to town.

Having made up his mind, Hughie began walking

away from town. He was heading west toward the Apache Indian reservation but he didn't even know the Indian Reservation was there. Hughie had arrived in Graneros from the east five years ago, walking along the dusty road. He'd been told to leave the orphan asylum where he'd grown up because he was too old to remain. He'd just started walking, living as best he could. When he arrived in Graneros Mr. Lockman gave him a job cleaning out the stable and the corrals in back of it. What had started out as a temporary job turned into a permanent one and Hughie stayed.

Hughie hadn't had many friends in his life because he was different, but Billy Pinto had been his friend. He wanted to go back to Graneros and tell the sheriff the names of the men who had hanged his friend.

If only fear had stood in the way, he might have gone. But there was something else. He didn't think he would be believed. When he accused those six important men of hanging Billy Pinto everybody was going to say he lied. They might even accuse him of killing Billy himself and put him in jail for it.

Thoroughly miserable, wanting to cry but feeling he was too old for it, Hughie plodded west.

# Chapter 3

It was seven o'clock when Thorpe Stedman left the restaurant. He'd eaten two thick slices of ham, three eggs, a stack of flapjacks, and had drunk two cups of coffee.

He crossed the street, angling toward the lower end of town where the livery stable was. Hughie Diggs ought to be hard at work by now. He usually arrived at the livery stable about six forty-five.

The place was deserted. Dave Lockman wasn't around but that wasn't surprising. He never arrived until after eight.

Frowning, Stedman stood in front of the stable several moments. Hughie Diggs was as reliable as the sun and a hell of a lot more punctual. He arrived at the stable at quarter of seven every morning and had for five years. He was never more than two or three minutes early, never more than two or three minutes late, variations probably explained by the inaccuracy of the clock at the boardinghouse.

The boardinghouse. He could find out if Hughie had eaten breakfast there. He mounted his horse and rode up Graneros Avenue to F Street and turned right. Mrs. Jorgensen's boardinghouse was located on the corner of F and First. It was a three-story frame, with lots of gabled windows on the upper story and scroll-work around the eaves. Next to the hotel, it was the largest building in town.

Stedman went around to the back. Mrs. Jorgensen heard him and came to the door. Stedman asked, "You seen Hughie this morning?"

She shook her head. "Something must have happened to that boy, Sheriff. He ain't never missed breakfast in all the five years he's been livin' here. He ain't never stayed out all night, either."

"Then he wasn't here at all last night?"

"No he wasn't. I went up to see why he didn't come to breakfast and his bed hadn't even been slept in."

Stedman nodded. He was beginning to get a little worried about Hughie now. Hughie's disappearance had to be connected with the hanging of Billy Pinto. He had the feeling he'd better find Hughie quickly if Hughie was still alive.

He rode back to Graneros Avenue and headed down toward the old stage station by the creek. Halfway to the creek, three horsemen came out of a side street in front of him. One was Ben Hurd. The second was Rufus Henshaw and the third was Max Steiner. They stopped their horses when they saw him and sat there waiting, trying not to look like kids caught with their hands in the cookie jar. All carried rifles.

Stedman asked, "Going hunting?"

There was a moment when confusion was apparent on the faces of all three. Then Henshaw said in a voice that almost squeaked, "We heard about Billy Pinto. We were going down there and see if we could pick up any tracks. We thought you were out of town."

"The hell! If you heard about Billy Pinto you should have heard that I was back. I was the one that found him hanging there."

Henshaw flushed. "Are you saying I'm a liar, Stedman?" His voice was trembling.

Stedman stared at him without replying. Henshaw looked away. Stedman said, "Go on home, the three of you. I'll take care of finding out who hanged Billy Pinto last night. If I need help, I'll call for it."

The three men turned their horses and rode back in the direction they had come. Stedman went on down the street, telling himself that at least he knew three of the men involved in the hanging the night before. And after he'd studied the tracks around the old stage station he'd know how many there had been besides the three.

The bridge sounded hollow beneath his horse's hoofs. He dismounted short of the gallows and proceeded on foot, studying the ground. There were a lot of tracks, those of his own horse among them. Patiently he studied the ground, sorting out each different set of tracks.

He finally decided that seven different men had been here last night. Apparently Billy Pinto had been led here on foot at the end of a rope. His run-down boot tracks overlaid the others, sometimes scuffed as if they were dragging him along.

Stedman began a slow, ever-widening circle around the gallows, until finally he picked up an eighth set of boot tracks, these being big work boots with the soles worn through.

Already he had spent almost an hour studying the ground. He guessed, and rightly, that this set of boot tracks belonged to Hughie Diggs. They had come toward the gallows and then had retreated, wide-spaced, indicating that Hughie had been running.

Now, overlying Hughie's tracks, Stedman found the tracks of a horse. The horse had pursued, plainly at a gallop, going right on past the place where Hughie had turned aside and lost himself in the dark. Out of curiosity, Stedman followed for a while. Apparently having become aware that he had lost Hughie in the dark, the rider had wandered around aimlessly for a while before returning to the old stage station where the others were.

Now Stedman took Hughie's trail. The boy had hidden in some brush, until his pursuer had gone by. Then he had climbed out of the bed of Conejos Creek. He had run blindly until he fell exhausted to the ground. His trail went on from there, heading west. Stedman followed it for several miles. It dropped into the bed of the creek again. Finally it went to a cave-like hole in the cutbank and, Stedman realized, this was where Hughie had spent the remainder of the night.

From the cutbank cave, the trail emerged. Hughie had started back toward town. He had hesitated, stopped, and finally had turned and headed west again.

Stedman kicked his horse's sides. Here, where the

29

trail was plain, he could follow at a steady trot.

It was now after nine o'clock. He continued traveling at a trot but even so it was forty-five more minutes before he sighted Hughie Diggs ahead.

He was a quarter mile behind Hughie when the boy finally turned and saw him coming. Immediately Hughie broke into a shambling run. Stedman kicked his horse into a lope, not because he was afraid of Hughie eluding him but because he saw no reason why the already terrified boy should exhaust himself in futile flight.

Boy. He always thought of Hughie as a boy, even though Hughie was probably twenty-four or -five. Hughie had simply not matured the way he would have if his mind had been a normally developed one.

Hughie was still trying to run when Stedman reached him. He rode his horse around in front of Hughie, forcing him to halt. Stedman said, "Whoa now. Whoa. I'm not going to hurt you, Hughie."

Hughie's eyes were filled with panic, like those of a rabbit cornered by a predator. He swallowed, choked, and finally managed to stammer, "I ain't done nothing. I ain't. Honest I ain't."

Stedman got down off his horse. Hughie looked as if he would run again, so Stedman didn't move toward him. As soothingly as he could he said, "I know you haven't, Hughie. I read the tracks. I know what happened back there last night."

Hughie was big, maybe six feet tall and he was muscular and strong from working around the livery barn.

His clothes were threadbare in spots and they weren't very clean. But they weren't the clothes he wore when he was working at the stable. Those clothes smelled so bad he kept them hanging on a nail at the livery barn. He wore these to the boardinghouse at night, probably because Mrs. Jorgensen wouldn't let him sit at the table otherwise.

His hair was tawny and needed cutting badly, and there were patches of yellow whiskers on his face that he had missed with his razor, which was never very sharp. His eyes were blue and contained some of the blank innocence of a very young animal.

Stedman said, "You were there last night when they hanged Billy Pinto. Did you see who they were?"

Pure terror now came to Hughie's eyes. He shook his head. "No, sir. I didn't see no faces. It was too dark."

Stedman knew he was lying and knew why. Hughie had the mistaken belief that if he refused to identify the lynchers his life would be safe. Stedman said, "Billy Pinto was your friend."

"Yes, sir."

"Don't you want to see the men who killed him pay for it?"

"It was dark. I didn't see nobody's face," Hughie insisted stubbornly.

Stedman nodded. He could pursue that later. Right now he wanted to know why Billy Pinto had been hanged. He asked, "Why did they do it, Hughie? Do you know?"

"They said . . ." Hughie's face suddenly went pale and his eyes took on that trapped and cornered look again. "You're tryin' to trick me. I said I didn't know who done that to him."

Stedman nodded. "All right, Hughie. Where you headed?"

There was more confusion in Hughie's face. Stedman said, "Just away, huh? Anywhere but Graneros."

Hughie nodded dumbly.

Stedman said, "I've got to take you back, Hughie."

Hughie looked behind him. His eyes were filled with panic as if he was going to run again. Stedman said, "It won't do any good. I've got a horse and I'll catch up with you." He saw the dumb fatalism that came to Hughie's eyes. It was like Hughie had accepted the idea that he was doomed, that he would be killed just as Billy Pinto had. Stedman got on his horse, rode to Hughie and gave him a stirrup. Hughie mounted behind him. Stedman didn't think Hughie would try overpowering him, but he took his revolver out of its holster anyway and stuffed it down in his belt in front. He turned the horse toward town.

For a while, the two rode in silence. Finally Stedman said, "I'm going to find out why Billy Pinto was hanged and I'm going to find out who did it. You can save me a lot of time and trouble if you'll tell me who it was."

There was only silence behind him.

Stedman said, "Three of them were starting out to

look for you this morning. Ben Hurd, Rufus Henshaw and Max Steiner." He turned his head and looked at Hughie's face.

It was almost green. For an instant, Stedman was afraid Hughie was going to jump off the horse and run again. He said, "So we know three of them. But I don't know why."

Hughie whispered, "Nobody's goin' to believe anythin' I say. I'm just ol' stupid Hughie Diggs and they is big important men."

"The court will believe you, Hughie, if you tell the truth." But Stedman wasn't so sure what he said was true.

"They wouldn't let me live that long. They'll kill me just like they killed Billy."

Stedman knew, suddenly, that he had no business taking Hughie Diggs back to Graneros at all. Hughie was right. They'd kill him whether he told their names or not. Because only if Hughie Diggs, the sole witness, was dead, could they feel safe.

# Chapter 4

There was only one place Stedman could put Hughie Diggs where he would be safe and that was in jail. When they reached it, he said, "Slide off, Hughie. And don't try to run. I'll catch you if you do."

Hughie slid off the horse's rump. Quickly, not quite trusting Hughie not to flee, Stedman dismounted.

With his eyes on Hughie, he tied his horse to the rail.

People all along the length of Graneros Avenue had stopped what they were doing to watch curiously. Stedman said, "Come on, Hughie." He walked to the jail door and unlocked the door.

Nervously, Hughie asked, "You going to put me in jail? I ain't done nothing wrong."

"I know you haven't, Hughie. But jail is the only place where you'll be safe."

"I got to get back to my job. I ain't never missed a day until today."

"I'll talk to Dave Lockman, Hughie. He won't fire you."

Hughie walked numbly to the jail door and stepped inside. Meekly he went through the door in back that led to the cells. There was an antiseptic odor in the air back there common to every jail Stedman had ever been inside. He said, "Take your pick, Hughie. Soon's I get you locked in, I'll get you something to eat."

Hughie went into a cell and Stedman locked the barred door behind him. Hughie looked confused and scared. Stedman said, "Don't worry, Hughie. It will turn out all right."

Hughie nodded but he didn't look any less scared. Stedman closed the door between the office and the cells, went out, and carefully locked the office door. He went down to the restaurant first, ordered a meal for Hughie and drank a cup of coffee while they got it ready for him. When it was ready, he carried it back, unlocked the door and took it to Hughie. Hughie didn't show much interest in the food so Stedman said, "Eat it, Hughie. It'll make you feel better."

"Yes, sir." Hughie obediently picked up the tray.

Stedman went out again, as carefully locking the door behind him. He mounted his horse and rode down Graneros Avenue to the livery stable. Dave Lockman was standing on the ramp that led in through the wide door watching him. He asked, "What's Hughie done?"

"Nothing he shouldn't have done. He just happened to see a hanging last night and he knows the men who did it."

Lockman's face was shocked. "Hanging? Here?"

Stedman was a little surprised that the whole town didn't already know about it. It must have been done pretty quietly, or late, or both. He said, "Billy Pinto."

"That Indian Hughie runs around with? What did he do?"

"That's what I'd like to find out. The reason I came over is that Hughie's afraid for his job. I told him I'd talk to you."

"You think they'd try getting rid of him to shut him up?"

Stedman shrugged. "They might. If they'd lynch Billy Pinto they wouldn't hesitate to kill the only witness that could pin it on them."

Lockman said, "You tell Hughie not to worry about his job. It'll be here when he gets out of jail."

Stedman looked at him gratefully. "Thanks."

"No thanks to me. It ain't easy to get somebody to

do the kind of work Hughie does an' be here every day to boot. Besides, I don't have to pay him much."

Stedman nodded. He rode on up Graneros Avenue to C Street and turned west to Second Street. He halted before a large brick building on the corner. A sign hung over the wide doors that said, WAGONER FURNITURE AND UNDERTAKING COMPANY. He thought that undertakers always seemed to be in the furniture business on the side. Or maybe it was the other way around. He supposed making furniture and coffins just naturally went together, requiring the same materials and skills.

A small door opened into the office on one side of the big door. Stedman tied his horse to the cast-iron hitching-post and went inside. Dallas Wagoner glanced up at him and the sheriff said, "We've got to bury Billy Pinto by tomorrow at the latest. Around ten-thirty suit you all right?"

Wagoner nodded. Stedman said, "I don't know what kind of service you'd have for an Indian. You know whether he was a Christian or not?"

"I doubt it. You aren't thinking about having a regular burial service for an Indian are you?"

Stedman stared coldly at him. "What would you suggest? You think we ought to ship him back to the Apaches?"

Wagoner's face suddenly was scared. "Good God, man, don't do that! No telling what those damned Apaches would do."

"All right then, let's have a burial. Just as if Billy

Pinto was human like you and me."

Dallas Wagoner flushed with anger. "No call to get nasty about it, Stedman. I only meant . . ."

"I know what you meant." Stedman turned and went outside.

He headed back downtown to the new stage depot half a block down from the jail. The telegraph office was next door to it. Sam Leonard, the telegrapher, looked up from a newspaper he was reading. Stedman said, "I want to send a message to the agent on the reservation."

Leonard got up and crossed the office to his instrument. Stedman wrote the message out on one of the yellow blanks. "Billy Pinto, Apache Indian living here, was hanged last night by persons unknown. Request you send a U.S. marshal soon as possible to assist investigation." He signed it, "Thorpe Stedman, Sheriff, Conejos County."

Leonard was as surprised as Dave Lockman had been at the news of Billy Pinto's death. Which cleared him in Stedman's mind. He paid for the telegram, took the stamped and receipted form, and tucked it into his shirt pocket so that he could be reimbursed for it.

He couldn't account for it rationally, but he had a sneaking hunch that Ben Hurd might be the one behind all this. Hurd had a sixteen-year-old daughter who was as fully developed as if she was twenty instead of sixteen. He headed for Ben Hurd's house.

It was almost noon. He saw Ben Hurd walking ahead of him, going home for dinner but he didn't hurry. He didn't want to catch up, because he wanted to watch Susan's face when he talked with Ben.

Hurd went up the alley and entered the back door. Stedman tied his horse in the alley, opened the gate and went to the back door. He knocked.

Hurd came to the kitchen door, crossed the screened-in porch, and stood looking at Stedman uncertainly. Stedman said, "I want to talk to you."

"All right. Go ahead." Hurd was wary.

Stedman heard Mrs. Hurd's voice. "Who is it, Ben?"

"It's the sheriff."

"What does he want?"

"Wants to talk to me."

"Well for heaven's sake, ask him to come in. Dinner's almost on the table. He'd just as well be eating while you two talk."

Hurd looked exceedingly uncomfortable but he was between a rock and a hard place and there was nothing he could do. He growled, "All right. Come on in."

Stedman felt a certain satisfaction at his discomfiture. As if the invitation was warm and genuine, he said, "Why thanks, Ben. That's mighty nice of Mrs. Hurd." He opened the screen door and crossed the porch to the kitchen door.

The place smelled of piccalilli, which Mrs. Hurd was canning now. The table was already set. Susan, sitting on the far side of it against the wall, did not look up as Stedman came in. He said, "Hello, Mrs. Hurd. Hello, Susan."

Mrs. Hurd smiled at him but there was an uneasy

quality to her smile. Susan shot him a quick glance and then as quickly looked down at her plate again. Ben Hurd said grudgingly, "You can sit here," and pulled out a chair.

Stedman sat down. Mrs. Hurd said, "Susan, help me put dinner on."

Hurd growled, "Let the girl alone," but Susan was already up. She carried a steaming dish of corn on the cob to the table. Her hands were trembling so violently as she put it down that it nearly overturned.

Hurd said, "Sit down, Susan. Your mother can put dinner on."

Susan sat down. Mrs. Hurd didn't say anything but her expression was both puzzled and confused. The atmosphere in the Hurd kitchen was charged with uneasiness. Stedman guessed that Mrs. Hurd knew nothing of what her husband had done last night, although she undoubtedly suspected that something was wrong.

Mrs. Hurd finished putting the serving dishes on. She sat down, bowed her head, and said grace. All four began to serve their plates. Stedman waited until everyone was served, mainly because he didn't want anybody dropping anything. Then he asked, "Did you hear about Billy Pinto, Mrs. Hurd?"

Hurd said protestingly, "Sheriff, not at the dinner table, if you please."

But Mrs. Hurd was curious. "What about Billy Pinto, Mr. Stedman?"

Stedman ignored Hurd's admonition. He said; "He

39

was hanged last night."

Mrs. Hurd's face turned pale with shock. "Hanged? You mean he's dead?"

"Yes, ma'am."

"What had he done? I didn't even know he was on trial."

"He wasn't, Mrs. Hurd. He was lynched. I don't even know yet what he was supposed to have done." He was studying Susan Hurd. Her face was turned down as much as she could turn it. Mostly hidden from him, it was almost gray. Her hand shook so violently that she dropped her fork and it clattered on her plate.

Her mother looked at her, "Susan, what on earth . . ."

Hurd said angrily, "I told you not to bring that up at the table, Sheriff. Now look what you've done. The girl's all upset."

Stedman met Hurd's angry glance. "You mean to tell me she didn't know?"

"Of course she didn't know! How could she know?"

Stedman said, "Susan?"

She refused to raise her glance. Her whole body was trembling now and she was gripping the edge of the table with both hands so tightly that her knuckles showed white.

There was a prolonged silence while nobody ate or moved. Finally Hurd said in a calming tone, "Eat your dinner, Susan. It's getting cold."

Suddenly, violently, Susan burst into tears. She got up from the table so precipitously that she overturned her chair. Her weeping was nearly hysterical as she fled the room.

For an instant, Ben Hurd and his wife stared at each other. Stedman studied both their expressions.

Mrs. Hurd was genuinely shocked but she was puzzled too. Hurd was angry but there was something else mixed with his anger. Stedman decided it could be guilt. Or something very close to it.

Mrs. Hurd got up. "Excuse me, Mr. Stedman. I think I had better go to her and find out what's wrong. Please finish your dinner."

She left the room. Stedman didn't feel like eating now but he forced himself. He wanted Hurd to think he was treating this as purely a family problem in which he had no part.

Hurd sat glaring at him as he ate, but Stedman pretended not to notice it. More than ever he was sure that Susan was the key to all that had happened in Graneros last night. And he could guess what that had been.

Hurd had caught Susan and Billy Pinto alone. Susan might either have been raped or she might have been a willing participant. The lack of any marks or bruises on her face tended to rule out assault.

There was only one thing wrong with that line of reasoning. It was totally impossible. He couldn't imagine Susan being interested in an Indian, much less a simple-minded one like Billy Pinto. And the idea of Billy Pinto trying to force Susan or anyone else was just plain unthinkable.

Both men could hear the voices of the two women faintly from another part of the house. Hurd kept looking toward the sound, back to Stedman, and then toward the sound again.

Stedman took the hint. He wiped his mouth with his napkin and got to his feet. "Thanks for the dinner, Ben. I hope nothing too serious is bothering Susan. I surely do."

Ben Hurd didn't speak. Before Stedman was across the porch he had left the kitchen; heading toward the sound of his wife's and Susan's voices.

Stedman walked slowly to where his horse was tied. He wanted to talk to Susan Hurd alone and he didn't quite know how he was going to manage it.

# Chapter 5

Thorpe Stedman did not return immediately to his office. The house of Ben Hurd sat alone on the bank of Conejos Creek and there was no way anybody could leave it without being seen. So he stationed himself behind a stable, itself behind the house of Rufus Henshaw, who was Hurd's closest neighbor. He dismounted, dropped the reins, and let his horse crop grass along the sides of the alley behind the stable. Feeling uncomfortable and a little guilty because he was spying, he hunkered down, put his back against the weathered boards of Henshaw's stable, and took a cigar from his pocket. He licked the dry and peeling wrapper, bit off the end, then stuck it into his mouth and lighted it. A light breeze carried the smoke away, dissipating it before it had gone half a dozen feet.

Guessing, he reconstructed in his mind what must have happened last night. Ben Hurd must have caught Susan with Billy Pinto, or with someone he thought was Billy Pinto. If there was any uncertainty over who it was it would mean that whoever it was had fled.

Stedman still could not believe Billy Pinto had been involved. He could not imagine Billy Pinto ever doing anything violent. He could not imagine him attacking and raping a white girl. But then, he had to admit, he hadn't known Billy. He'd only nodded or spoken to him occasionally. He had never even heard the sound of Billy's voice.

In any case, Billy Pinto had been blamed. Maybe he had been guilty. Maybe he had been seen and recognized. Or maybe Susan had named him as her attacker.

Stedman didn't even feel sure it had been an attack. He had not been blind to the way Susan paraded herself on Graneros Avenue. Having been caught, she might have just claimed to have been forced. She could not have foreseen the consequences. Hearing that Billy Pinto had been hanged must have come as a terrible shock to her.

Shock enough to make her behave the way she had a while ago at the dinner table. Shock enough to make her flee the room in tears.

All right, he told himself, use your own best judgment and reconstruct what happened from the facts you have. He went on and what he came up with was surprisingly accurate even though he didn't know it was.

Susan had been with somebody all right, but it had been a white boy, not Billy Pinto, and it had not been rape. Caught with Susan by her father, the boy had fled into the darkness. Terrified, Susan had claimed she was attacked to escape her father's wrath. The name of Billy Pinto had come swiftly to her mind because she knew her father would be more than willing to believe it of an Indian.

Ben Hurd's actions had been predictable from that point on. He had solicitously accompanied Susan back to the house, relieved that she wasn't seriously hurt. Then he had gone to round up some of his friends.

It hadn't been hard to convince them that Billy Pinto had taken Susan by force. It hadn't been hard to talk them into making Billy Pinto pay. They had gone out, in a group, found Billy Pinto and dragged him to the gallows across Conejos Creek. In his terror, Billy had probably forgotten every English word he knew, and they wouldn't have believed anything he said anyway. He was an Indian, wasn't he? He had been accused by a white girl, Ben Hurd's daughter, who had to be respected and believed.

Some of the men might have had second thoughts about the actual lynching. But they had been overruled. Billy Pinto had been hanged.

Stedman's eye caught movement over at Ben Hurd's house. He saw Hurd come from the back door, pause to pack and light his pipe, then walk toward town. He followed Hurd with his glance until Hurd disappeared. He continued to wait, knowing it might be a long wait, knowing Susan might not appear at all before he had to give this vigil up and return to the jail.

Half an hour passed. The cigar butt had long since been ground out beneath his heel. He was just rising to leave when he heard the slam of the Hurds' back porch screen.

Glancing that way, he saw Susan, poised on the stoop. She glanced to right and left, almost like a frightened animal. Then she ducked down into the bed of Conejos Creek, disappearing from Stedman's view.

Instantly he hurried to his horse and mounted him. He rode to the cutbank leading down into the creekbed, and glanced right and left. He saw Susan, running, holding her skirts up so that she wouldn't trip over them.

He dug his horse with his heels and the animal slid down the cutbank into the bed of the creek. Stedman let him trot, maintaining the same distance behind Susan, wondering where she was going in such a hurry. If he'd had to guess, he'd have said to the boy's house. The boy who had been with her last night.

Considering it, he decided he didn't really want to know who the boy had been. Nor did he want Ben Hurd to know. Hurd had already done enough.

He kicked his horse into a lope. He overtook Susan rapidly, but not until he was fifty yards behind did she hear him, stop and turn.

Even at this distance he could see the uncertainty in her. She didn't know whether to run or stay. Finally her shoulders slumped. Apparently she had decided she couldn't escape no matter how she tried.

There was defiance in her eyes and resentment on her face as he reached her and swung to the ground. He said, "I'm glad you're not so upset any more. I want to talk to you."

Now she was sullen. "What about?"

"About last night."

Fear came to her eyes, visible before she once more looked at the ground. Still sullenly she asked, "What about last night?"

"I want to know what happened."

"Happened?" She glanced up quickly, trying to look both puzzled and surprised.

"Yes, happened. Last night. I want to know what happened to make your father do what he did."

Her expression showed that she suspected even if she wasn't sure. That her father had helped hang Billy Pinto. That it was her fault that he had. Her false accusation had doomed Billy Pinto and that made her guilty of his death.

Her eyes brimming, she looked up at him. He had never seen a more terrible expression or more suffering on a human face. He said, "I'm sorry, Susan, but I've got to know."

She began to shake as if she had some terrible kind of chill. Her face contorted. And suddenly she crumpled to the ground, assuming a kind of hunkered position in which her head was encircled by her arms, her face buried in her knees. Wild hysteria took her and sobs seemed torn out of her. That violent trembling continued and Stedman had the uneasy feeling that he had gone too far. He said, "Susan? Susan?" helplessly, not knowing what to do. Thorpe Stedman hadn't had much experience with women. His mother died when he was four and he'd grown up in a man's world. He'd known his share of saloon women, of course, and Serena Van Vleet, but that was about it. Except for line-of-duty contacts with the married women of the town.

Susan's wild weeping continued until he thought she'd never stop. Finally he hunkered down beside her, not touching her. He said, "Let me tell you how I think it was. You and some boy were together last night. Your father caught you and the boy ran away. You were scared of what your father would do to you so you lied. You said it had been Billy Pinto and you said you had been forced."

Her trembling stopped. She was, for a moment, silent, motionless. Finally a long, shuddering sob escaped her lips. Her voice was like a cry, "I didn't know he'd do it! I didn't know!"

He said, "I know you didn't. How *could* you know?"

She raised her head. Her face was streaked with tears, her eyes red from weeping. "What am I going to do?"

Thorpe Stedman shook his head. He couldn't tell her because he didn't know. A terrible thing had been

47

done last night and there were going to be terrible consequences. A human life had been taken unlawfully and unjustly and those who had taken it had to pay.

Stedman asked, "Where were you going now? To see the boy?"

She nodded numbly, opened her mouth to speak. Stedman said quickly, "No! I don't want to know who it was."

Again she wailed, "What am I going to do?"

He said, "Go on back home."

"Will my father have to go to jail?"

"Probably."

Her weeping began anew. "It's my fault. If I hadn't lied . . ."

Stedman said firmly, "It's not your fault. Your father didn't have to do what he did. He could have come to me."

"But if it hadn't been for me . . ."

"Putting blame isn't going to help. Stop crying now and go home." He made his voice firm, despite his sympathy for the tortured girl.

"Yes, sir." He lifted her to her feet and watched her stumble back in the direction she had come, toward home. Then he mounted his horse and rode back toward the jail.

He felt terribly sorry for Susan Hurd. She had done nothing hundreds, maybe thousands of girls before her had not done. But she had been caught and in her fright she had lied to spare herself the punishment she knew was coming to her.

Because her father was who he was and what he was, and because her choice of a man to accuse had been unfortunate, terrible consequences had ensued. The fact that Billy Pinto had been an Indian was going to involve a federal agency, and probably the federal courts as well.

Sourly, Stedman cursed to himself. He was the middleman. It was his duty to enforce the law, to find and arrest every man who had been involved in the hanging last night. Six men. Their trials would inevitably involve the whole territory. Malcontents on the reservation might seize on the lynching of Billy Pinto to break out and renew hostilities against the whites. It could even result in another Indian war.

He was glad he had asked for a U.S. marshal. At least if a marshal came, he wouldn't have to handle this alone.

He dismounted in front of the jail. The street looked normal for this time of day except that people seemed to have gathered into small groups to talk. As he unlocked the door of the jail, he could feel everybody watching him.

He went in, closing the door behind. He shook down the ashes in the stove. He stuck his head through the door leading to the cells. "Want some coffee, Hughie?"

"Yes, sir."

Stedman built a fire. He added water and coffee to the pot and put it on. He sat down, thinking that he was going to have to get the names of the six men who had hanged Billy Pinto out of Hughie soon. He already knew who three of them were but he had to know them all.

# Chapter 6

Ben Hurd was shaking violently when he left the house. It didn't even occur to him to look and see if anyone was watching him. He was consumed by the fearful thoughts churning in his head. He was convinced that Stedman knew why Billy Pinto had been hanged last night, knew he had instigated it and knew Susan was the cause.

But damn it, he reasoned desperately, a man had a right to defend his womenfolks. His daughter particularly. Holy God, Susan was only sixteen years old. For a dirty damn Indian to defile her the way Billy Pinto had . . . The stinking Indian had deserved to die.

Self-justification was difficult to sustain. Fear was too strong. No matter what justification a man had, the law didn't permit him to hang another human being, regardless of what that other human being had done. Not even an Indian. And Stedman being the kind of man he was, would dig away at this until he knew the name of every one of the six who had participated.

Hurd was under no illusions about the men who had helped him hang the Indian. When Stedman arrested them, they'd fall all over themselves blaming him. They'd say he had instigated the whole thing. They'd say that, until the last moment, they'd thought it was only meant to throw a good scare into the Indian. They'd even claim Pinto's death was an accident that happened because the scare got out of hand.

If the jury believed them, then the brunt of the whole thing would fall on him. He would be the goat. He would be the one who went either to the gallows or to prison for the rest of his life. The Tucson and Albuquerque newspapers would get hold of it, and the law would need a scapegoat. Which would end up being him.

Unless there wasn't any proof. Unless there was no one to testify and name names. Unless Hughie Diggs was silenced. For good. They should have gotten him last night. Having failed that, they had better get him today.

By the time he reached Graneros Avenue, he was almost running. He was sweating heavily. Nothing like this had ever happened to him before and he was scared.

He wouldn't have admitted it, but more than fear was troubling him. For one thing, it was peculiar that Susan had no marks on her, no apparent injuries. Her hysteria, today hours after the attack, further troubled him. It seemed to have been caused by Stedman's statement that Billy Pinto had been hanged last night. It was likely she hadn't known about the hanging earlier. Plenty of people in Graneros didn't know. But why should it send her into hysteria? You'd think she'd be glad that he was dead, that she didn't have to get up in court and tell what he had done to her, that she wouldn't have people staring and pointing their fingers at her.

He went first to Rufus Henshaw's gunsmith shop at the lower end of Graneros Avenue. Henshaw was just returning from dinner and still had his hat on. He looked at Hurd when he came in as if he wished he had never seen him before. Hurd said, "Stedman's got Hughie Diggs in jail."

"I know it." Henshaw was a slight man, wearing gold-rimmed glasses pinched to his nose. His hands, which could do the most intricate engraving on the receiver of a gun, were shaking so badly now they wouldn't have been able to hold an engraving tool.

"Do you suppose he's talked yet? He will, if we don't shut him up."

"We can't . . . I mean we've already killed one man." Henshaw looked as if he was going to be sick.

"You want to hang like Billy Pinto did? Or would you rather spend the rest of your life in Yuma?"

"If I'd known . . . Oh God, I wish we hadn't. . . ."

Hurd said brutally, "Well, we did." Inside he was as scared as Henshaw was but he didn't dare let it show. "We did and we'll pay for it unless we get rid of Hughie Diggs. It ain't as if he was . . . well, the same as everybody else." That was the technique. You first demean and de-humanize the person you intend to kill. That makes it easier.

Henshaw was almost whispering as he asked, "What do you want me to do?"

"Meet with us. Up at my store in half an hour. Come up the alley and in the back door so's you won't be seen. We'll all decide what to do. If we stick together, we'll be all right."

Henshaw looked doubtful but he agreed. Hurd went back out. He went to Max Steiner's hardware store next. Steiner took what Hurd had to say a lot more calmly than Henshaw had. He even agreed to see Martin Watts and give him the message that they were to meet at Hurd's store in half an hour.

Hurd went to the Red Dog Saloon next because he knew that was where he'd find Peter Judd. Peter was Serena Van Vleet's brother. He was almost thirty and he did a better job of living without working than anybody Hurd had ever seen. He'd gotten in on the lynching by accident. He'd just happened on them as they were dragging Billy Pinto down the street.

Judd was sitting in a corner playing solitaire with a dog-eared deck of greasy cards. Hurd sat down. "Stedman's got Hughie Diggs in jail and Hughie knows every one of us. We're having a meeting up at my store in half an hour."

Peter was a tall, slender, good-looking man with a wide mustache and a short goatee that pretty well managed to hide the weakness in his face. He was very successful with the ladies and wasn't above taking money from them, "loans" that they were later too ashamed to report. He had gone along with the lynch party last night just for the excitement of it. Now his expression said he wished that he had not. He nodded and casually played a red seven on a black eight but his hands shook badly enough to give him away.

Hurd left, thinking that the fact that Thorpe Stedman was sweet on Peter's sister might possibly help somewhere along the line. Stedman would be in a hell of a position when he found out Peter was involved in the hanging. He couldn't let Peter go without letting all of them go. And he would probably lose Serena if he threw her brother in jail on a murder charge.

Curtis Redding was the only one who remained. He was the printer. He got out the Graneros *Gazette* once a month. It had a circulation of less than a hundred, including the ranches and smaller towns in the county. Redding was a bachelor, under thirty. He wouldn't have helped last night except for the fact that he'd been kind of sweet on Susan. He always watched her walking along the street from the window of his shop with hungry eyes. Maybe he'd been waiting until she was older to start courting her. Maybe he'd just been too shy. But the news that she'd been raped by a dirty Indian had infuriated him enough to make him come along. Afterward, when Billy Pinto was swinging there, he had run off into the darkness and gotten sick.

Hurd said, "Stedman has got Hughie Diggs down at the jail. Hughie can name every one of us. We're having a meeting at my store in half an hour to decide what to do about him."

"Do about him?" Redding looked as if he'd like to run. "What do you mean, do about him?"

"I mean we can't let him name names in court. I mean we'd better figure some way of shutting him up."

Redding's voice was a hoarse whisper. "You mean kill him, don't you?"

Hurd lost patience. "I mean any goddamned thing that's necessary. Unless we want to hang or unless we want to go to Yuma for the rest of our lives."

Redding nodded weakly. "All right, I'll come. But no more killing. There's got to be a way to do it without killing him."

Hurd withheld the sarcastic remark he felt like making. He said, "Come in the back door."

"All right."

Hurd went out, slamming the door unnecessarily hard behind him. Angrily he marched up the street. Damn them! Damn them! They'd feel differently if it had been their daughter who'd been raped by that dirty Indian.

He fueled his anger with his indignation but it was becoming harder and harder all the time. Susan's lack of bruises or marks nagged his mind. So did her hysteria when she heard that Billy Pinto had been lynched. Was it possible that Susan had lied to him, that Billy Pinto hadn't been the man? Was it even possible that it had not been rape at all?

Furiously he put the disquieting thoughts out of his head. He reached his store and went inside. Middle-aged Mrs. Brackett, his clerk, was waiting on a customer. As he went past her, Hurd said, "I've got some

55

bookwork to do out back. I don't want to be disturbed."

"Yes, sir, Mr. Hurd." He went on down the long aisle to the back room. He closed the door behind him and shot the bolt. He had a small office in one corner of the back room. The rest of it was occupied by piled-up merchandise.

Henshaw, Steiner and Peter Judd were already there. Hurd led them to his office. There weren't enough chairs for them so they got boxes from outside the office and brought them in. Redding and Watts came in together.

Hurd looked around at the faces of the five other men. He said, "You all know about Hughie Diggs. Something's got to be done and done tonight unless we either want to hang or spend the rest of our lives in Yuma. I guess we'd better decide what it's going to be."

Redding, white-faced but determined, said, "You got us into this. If it hadn't been for you . . ."

Hurd interrupted. "You two-faced son-of-a-bitch, you were anxious enough to go last night. I've seen the way you look at Susan. The only thing that made you mad was that somebody else got to her first!"

Redding's face turned a painful red. He looked at his feet. Steiner said, "Hey now, let's don't get to fighting among ourselves. We all went and we all took part. Now we've got to decide, all together, what's to be done."

Redding looked up. It was painful for him because

what Hurd had said was the truth. But there was stubborn determination in his thin face and in his scared blue eyes. He said, "No more killing. I won't be a part of any more killing no matter what they do to me."

Hurd glared at him. He knew that unless he shut Redding up, the man might end up influencing some of the others. He said, "The rest of us don't feel that way, you yellow-bellied skunk! Just you remember that we're all fighting for our lives. Hughie Diggs has got to go because he can identify every one of us. If you don't want to go along with it, then maybe, by God, you'll have to go too."

Anger touching his voice now, Henshaw said, "I thought this was a meeting to decide what we ought to do. Looks to me like the two of you have already decided without even giving the rest of us a say."

Hurd growled, "All right, have your say."

Henshaw looked at Steiner. "What do you say, Max?"

Steiner frowned. It was plain that he wasn't partial to the idea of killing Hughie Diggs. He said, "Hughie ought to scare easy. What if we was to tell him to keep his mouth shut or we'd shut it for him, permanently?"

Judd shook his head. "Huh uh. Hughie's not too bright. You all know that. Stedman will find a way of getting it out of him without Hughie even realizing he's spilling anything."

Martin Watts, the town carpenter, nodded his graying head. "He's right. Stedman will get it out of him some way. We can't count on Hughie's being still."

Redding said, faintly but firmly, "No."

Hurd swung without thinking. The flat of his hand struck the side of Redding's face with a sound like a pistol shot. A red mark, the shape of Hurd's hand, appeared almost instantly on Redding's ashen face. His eyes began to water from the pain, but his mouth lost none of its stubborn set. He was scared but he wasn't going to back off.

Steiner said, "That kind of thing isn't going to get us together. I say let's break this up and go home and cool off a little. We can't do anything until it gets dark anyhow. Let's think about it and meet again right after supper. Maybe by then we can look at this thing sensibly."

Hurd opened his mouth to argue, closed it without saying anything. Steiner was right. They weren't going to reach an agreement now and all the shouting and name calling in the world wouldn't change that fact. Hurd instinctively knew that if he pushed Redding any further, Steiner and Henshaw were likely to join with him in opposition to killing Hughie Diggs. But if the three of them had time to think, maybe they'd see that it was the only way.

He said, "All right. Where do you want to meet?"

Steiner said, "This is as good a place as any. Let's meet right here. About eight-thirty tonight."

All the men seemed glad to leave. Hurd watched them file out the back door into the alley.

He stood there for what seemed a long, long time. He didn't feel like waiting on customers today. He just wanted to be alone. He wanted a chance to sort his own thoughts out and he wanted a chance to try and find some other solution to the problem facing the six of them. He didn't want to kill Hughie Diggs any more than Redding did. He was more realistic, that was all.

Sure that all the others had by now disappeared, he unlocked the door leading from the storeroom to the store. Then he stepped out the back door into the alley, starting violently with surprise when he saw Thorpe Stedman standing not a dozen feet away.

## Chapter 7

For an instant, the two men stared at each other in surprise. Then, recovering, Ben Hurd scowled. "What the hell are you doing here?"

Had he not known the strain Ben Hurd was under, the question might have irritated Stedman, who had every right to be in this alley or any other one. He said, "I wanted to see you."

"What's the matter with the front door?"

Stedman shrugged. "Nothing, I guess. I just thought that what I had to say ought to be said in private."

"And what would that be?" Hurd was studying Stedman's expression closely, trying to guess whether or not Stedman had seen the others leaving here. His guess was that Stedman had not, unless he had been watching the back door or the store for some time.

Stedman said, "Your daughter wasn't raped."

Raw fury flooded Hurd, who already had his back to the wall and who had, deep in his heart, suspected this. Trembling, hands clenched into fists, he said, "You son-of-a-bitch, you'd better have proof of that or, sheriff or not, I'll beat you to a pulp!"

Stedman didn't bother to discuss proof because he could see it wasn't needed. Hurd must already have suspected that Susan had not been raped. Instead Stedman said, "Billy Pinto wasn't even involved. You and the others hanged the wrong man." Putting it into words angered him. Because one man, Ben Hurd, had gone off half cocked and taken the law into his own hands, a man was dead, six men were murderers and the trouble sure as hell wasn't over yet. While Ben Hurd stood there, stunned into immobility, he repeated with savage anger, "You hanged the wrong man, did you hear? It was somebody else and it wasn't rape. Your daughter was scared of you and she lied."

A wordless roar broke from Ben Hurd's mouth. This was precisely what some inner voice had been telling him. He hadn't believed it because he couldn't bear to believe. But now he had no choice. It had come from the lips of the sheriff and he knew the sheriff had to have heard it from Susan herself.

Furiously he rushed, his arms flailing wildly. By his momentum he bore the sheriff back, and slammed him against a crumbling board fence on the far side of the alley. One of his fists happened to connect with Stedman's mouth, smashing lips, bringing a rush of blood as Stedman nearly bit off the end of his tongue.

Stedman was, for the moment, pinned against the fence, half prone, half erect. Hurd was a wild man, swinging his arms and fists with no direction and no skill, but connecting often enough to keep Stedman from recovering his feet or fighting back.

Still surprised at the savagery of the attack, Stedman absorbed the furious blows that landed, finally abandoning his attempts to make it back to his feet and letting himself slide down the fence into a sitting position instead. One of Hurd's clenched fists struck a fence post squarely with all the force of which he was capable and he howled and held it up in front of him like the broken wing of a bird while he stared at it in disbelief.

Stedman took advantage of the instant's respite to roll, scramble a few feet on hands and knees, and then come to his feet. Hurd turned to face him, driven even wilder by the nearly unbearable pain in his hand. He rushed again, as if by obliterating Stedman he could obliterate not only the pain but also the truth that Stedman had uttered a few moments before.

Stedman had never seen a man lose control of himself so completely. He knew of no way of stopping Hurd and he didn't want to engage in a brawl with him yet he had no intention of making matters worse by using his gun. He stepped aside nimbly and Hurd, expecting anything but this, went past, carried by his own momentum, to stumble over a board that had come off the fence and go crashing to the ground.

Stedman spit a mouthful of blood into the alley dust, wondering how long it was going to take for Hurd's fury to exhaust itself. He could have clipped the man with the barrel of his gun, or he could have kicked him in the head, yet he did neither. Hurd had hanged Billy Pinto wrongfully. He had made killers of five other men who were his friends. And yet, Stedman couldn't help feeling sorry for the man, and he didn't want to hurt him more.

Hurd got up. He was dusty, bloody, and panting. His eyes were bloodshot, the veins in his forehead and neck distended. He was trembling violently. Stedman was suddenly grateful that Hurd did not have a gun.

He knew he ought to put Hurd under arrest. He told himself he did not because he had no proof of what Hurd had done last night, no proof that would hold up in court. But that wasn't the reason. The real reason was that he suspected he'd have to risk killing Hurd if he tried to arrest him now. Hurd wanted to go home. He wanted to confront Susan and he wanted to be told the truth. From Susan's own lips.

Stedman said soothingly, "Go home, Ben. Talk to Susan. But don't be too hard on her. She was scared and she's still only a kid. Kids tell lies when they're scared."

Hurd did not reply. He reminded Stedman in that moment of an old bull, tormented beyond belief, who had charged his tormenters and charged and charged again until he was too exhausted to charge any more. Stedman repeated, "Go home, Ben," and turned his back. He didn't know whether Hurd would attack him but he was prepared to take the chance in the hope of breaking the encounter off. He went fifty yards before he turned his head.

Hurd was stumbling up the alley in the other direction as if he was in a daze. As Stedman watched, he cut between two buildings and through a vacant lot toward the street.

Stedman fished a bandanna from his pocket and mopped at his bleeding mouth. He'd have a tongue so sore he'd have trouble eating for several days. His mouth would swell up so that everybody who saw him would know he had been in a fight.

He hoped Hurd would take his advice and not be too hard on Susan, but he didn't believe Hurd would. Hurd had made a terrible mistake, one that might well ruin his entire life and the lives of the members of his family. He wasn't likely to be reasonable when he confronted Susan, whose lie had started everything.

Angrily, because this all was so unnecessary, Stedman headed for the jail. He wanted the names of the other five and he wanted them from Hughie's lips. He wanted some evidence that he could make arrests on and take into court.

He reached C Street and turned toward Graneros Avenue. For the town of Graneros, the street was crowded, with women, children, men. Stedman suddenly realized how he looked. He was covered with dust. The front of his shirt was spattered with blood and his face probably was too. He didn't want people to see him like this and he couldn't get into the jail to clean up without being seen because it had no back door.

He thought of Serena Van Vleet. He could go to her place. He could clean up there. Better still, he could talk to her. He could get some of the things that were worrying him off his chest.

He turned and headed toward Second Street. Serena lived in a small, white-framed house on Second between D and E. He reached the front gate and went through.

She must have seen him coming because the door was open when he climbed the two steps to the porch. "For heaven's sake, what happened to you? Are you hurt?"

He shook his head, grinning crookedly because of his swelling lips. "Just a little dirty and bloody is all. Do you mind if I clean up here?"

"Of course not. Come in."

He went in, noticing how nice she smelled as he went past. He'd have bent his head and given her a light kiss in passing except for his bloody mouth. She seemed to expect it and stood poised a moment, waiting. When he went on she closed the door and followed him through to the kitchen.

She poured some warm water into a basin from a tea-kettle on the stove, then got him a washcloth and a towel. She said, "I wondered why I kept my husband's old shirts. Now I know. I'll get you one." She left the room.

Stedman washed his face and hands and dabbed gingerly at his bleeding mouth with the damp washcloth. Still doing it, he went out onto the back porch and brushed off his pants with his hands as best he could. He took off his shirt when he saw Serena coming with the clean one, took it from her, and put it on. It was a little tight, but not too much so. Serena buttoned it for him while he continued to dab at his bleeding mouth.

There was something stirring about having her stand there buttoning his shirt. Their glances locked and something unmistakable passed between them. She stood there, waiting for a moment as if expecting him to say something. When he did not, she stepped back and said, "Well, tell me what happened to you. Who were you fighting with?" There was a light and teasing quality to her voice but her eyes turned grave when she saw the expression on his face. She asked, "Is it something to do with that awful thing last night?"

Stedman nodded. Serena said, "Come sit down and tell me about it."

That was exactly what he wanted. He followed her through the kitchen and into the small parlor that opened off her sewing room. He said, "Ben Hurd caught his daughter with somebody last night. She was scared and she claimed it had been Billy Pinto and that he took her by force."

"But it wasn't true?"

"No. I don't know who it was, but Susan wasn't forced. Anyhow, Ben Hurd flew off the handle. Everybody hates Indians around here and the thought of an Indian touching his daughter must have made him wild. He got five others to help him and the bunch of them dragged Billy Pinto down to that old stage station and strung him up. I found him on my way into town last night."

"Were you fighting with Mr. Hurd? Did you arrest him?"

He shook his head. "Not yet. It seems that Hughie Diggs was in the stage station last night while the hanging was going on. Maybe he followed them after they grabbed Billy Pinto or maybe he just happened to be there. I don't know. But he saw all six of the men and they saw him. He got away. I trailed him and brought him back. But he's scared to talk and until he does I can't arrest anyone."

"Then what was the fight about?"

"I guess I told Ben something he didn't want to hear. That Susan wasn't forced. And that he hanged the wrong man."

"Where is he now?" Despite the terrible thing Hurd had done, her face showed her compassion for the man.

"Went home to get the truth out of Susan."

"That poor child!"

"That poor child is responsible for everything that's happened."

"But she didn't mean any harm. She was frightened and she lied. Didn't you ever try to lie yourself out of

66

something when you were a boy?"

Stedman grinned with his swollen lips. He nodded. Serena said, "Do you have to handle this all alone? Can't you get some help?"

"I've wired for a U.S. marshal. The murder of an Indian is the business of the federal government."

She was sitting beside him on the sofa. Now she put a hand out and laid it on top of his. He said, "I guess I didn't come here just to get cleaned up. I guess I needed somebody to talk to."

She smiled. Suddenly and without even thinking about what he was saying, he asked, "When are you going to marry me?"

For a moment her eyes were startled. Then she smiled and the smile spread until she was laughing. A little huffily Stedman asked, "What's so funny about that?"

"You just took me by surprise, asking me when. You've never even asked me before."

"Well, I'm asking you now."

She moved closer to him, took his face between her hands, and pulled it down until she could kiss him lightly on his bruised and bleeding mouth. She said, "I'll marry you whenever you want me to."

"You will?" It was a silly remark but it just slipped out. Serena was still smiling gently. She said, "I was beginning to think you'd never ask. You're not regretting it already, are you?"

Stedman smiled ruefully. "Surprised at myself is all. I've been thinking about asking you, but I hadn't planned to do it now. It just slipped out." That wasn't strictly true. He had been thinking about her do-nothing brother and wondering how it would work out, being the brother-in-law of someone he so thoroughly disliked. But he doubted if many marriages began without problems of some kind or other.

He got up. "I suppose I'd better be getting back. Thanks for letting me clean up and for the shirt."

She came to him and he put his arms around her and pulled her close. With her body warm against him all his doubts and nervousness disappeared. He said, "As soon as this business is over with, we'll go away."

She was smiling and her eyes clung to his. He wondered why he hadn't asked her to marry him a long time ago.

# Chapter 8

Ben Hurd was still furious when he reached home, more so because he knew in his heart that everything the sheriff had said was true. He slammed the porch door and flung open the kitchen door so hard that he smashed the glass in it. Broken shards of it tinkled to the floor.

His wife was in the kitchen. She turned a startled and terrified glance toward him, gulped and managed to get out the words, "Ben, what in the world . . . ?"

"Where is she?" he roared. "Where's Susan?"

"In her room, I suppose. The sheriff telling about

that hanging upset her."

"It ought to," he snapped, "seein' she caused it!"

"Caused it? Whatever are you talking about?" Mrs. Hurd's face was white, her eyes filled with fear of this thing she could not yet comprehend.

"Never mind!" He stalked across the kitchen, through the dining room and to the foot of the stairs. Behind him, Mrs. Hurd followed, a dish towel in her hands. Standing at the foot of the stairs, Ben bellowed, "Susan! Get down here!"

Waiting, he paced furiously back and forth while Mrs. Hurd looked on, nervously wiping her hands with the towel, over and over even though they were by now completely dry. No sound came from upstairs, so Ben bellowed again, "Susan!"

The bed finally creaked in Susan's room. The stairs squeaked as she came down, slowly, fearfully.

Her face, when she reached the foot of the stairs, was ghastly. Ben gave her no time to compose herself. "Who was it?" he bellowed. "Who?"

She made a feeble attempt at misunderstanding him, her last defense. "What do you mean, Papa? Who was who?"

"Goddamn it, you know what I mean!" Before he could go on, Mrs. Hurd interjected timidly, automatically and from habit, "Ben, your language!"

"To hell with that!" he roared. "Who was it? Who was it with you last night?"

Susan's eyes looked like those of a rabbit trapped by a coyote. Ben shouted, "Damn it, who?"

She couldn't speak. She was so terrified her throat had closed. She tried to swallow and fought to do so for several seconds while it looked as if she was going to choke. At last Ben roared, "It wasn't that Indian, was it? It wasn't Billy Pinto at all?"

Numbly she shook her head. Her eyes looked as if she thought he would kill her then and there.

The answer seemed to stun Ben Hurd because it told him, finally and unequivocally, that he had murdered an innocent man. As quickly as it had come, his anger disappeared. His face turned a sickly shade of green and he looked as if he was going to be sick. In a voice that didn't even sound like his own, he asked, "You weren't forced, either, were you? You were out there rolling on the ground with him because you wanted to."

Mrs. Hurd broke in. "Ben Hurd, don't you talk to your daughter that way!"

He looked numbly at his wife. "Do you know what she did?"

Mrs. Hurd shook her head. Her expression said that in her heart she knew but as yet nobody had put it into words.

In a voice that was monotonous and devoid of expression, Hurd said, "She had someone out there with her last night. She was rolling in the dirt with him. When I came along, he got up and ran and left her there. She told me she was forced and she told me it was that Indian, Billy Pinto, who forced her."

Mrs. Hurd looked at her daughter with shocked

eyes. "Susan! How could you do such a thing?"

Susan didn't reply. She was swaying, as if she was going to faint.

Hurd went on. "Thinking about that dirty Indian forcing my daughter drove me wild. I went out and got some friends together. I thought I was doing right, I swear to God I did. I thought I was protecting all the women and girls that live in this town."

Mrs. Hurd's voice was a whisper and her face was nearly as sick as Susan's was. "*You* hanged him, didn't you?"

He nodded, unable now to speak.

Mrs. Hurd seemed to forget that Susan was in the room. She came to her husband and put her hands on his arms while she looked up into his face, her eyes brimming with tears. "Oh, Ben, I'm sorry."

He put his arms around her and held her so tightly that her face contorted with pain. But she did not cry out.

Ben Hurd's body convulsed. It began with a shaking, as if he had a chill. Then, after the shaking had grown nearly uncontrollable, a single sob was wrenched from him. And then he broke completely and wept like a heartbroken child.

Terrified, shocked beyond belief, Susan crept up the stairs and back to her room. Desperately she wished that she was dead.

She deserved to die, she thought numbly. Look at what she had done to her father. Look at what she had done to Billy Pinto, who had done nothing wrong.

Look at the suffering her mother was going through and at the consequences facing those who had helped her father hang Billy Pinto last night.

Her father and mother's room was at the front of the house, down a long hall. Silently she crept along that hall until she reached the door of their room. Silently she opened it and went inside.

In a corner of the closet her hand touched something hard and cold. She withdrew it, her father's double-barreled shotgun that he used for hunting ducks.

She knew where he kept the shells. She got a couple of them out of the drawer and broke the gun the way she'd seen her father do. She put the shells in and closed the gun with a snap. She pulled back both hammers with fingers that trembled so badly she had trouble making them do what she wanted them to do.

She could still hear the awful sounds of her father's weeping down at the foot of the stairs, could hear her mother's soothing, comforting voice. The world, which had seemed so beautiful and exciting only yesterday was now a cold and ugly place where there was no hope.

She put the barrel of the gun against her head and reached for the trigger with one hand while the other held the gun steady against her head. In an instant it would be over. Her blood would spatter the walls and ceiling of this room. Her body would crumple lifeless to the floor.

Her death wouldn't solve her father's problem, of

course. But it might make things go easier for him at the trial.

Her forefinger touched one of the triggers. All she needed to do now was push slightly against it. The hammer would fall and the gun would leap as if it was alive. Susan wouldn't hear the blast. She wouldn't feel anything. She would be dead instantly.

She tried to push against the trigger, tried to apply the slight pressure, which was all that it would take, but she could not. The vision of her blood spattered on the walls and ceiling, of her lying on the floor with her head nearly blown apart, was more than she could stand.

She took the gun muzzle away from her head. She laid the gun on the bed. She returned on tiptoe to her room.

Outside her window was the back porch roof. She crawled out the window and tiptoed across it to a tree that grew at its corner. She stepped from the porch into the tree and climbed down to the ground.

She hurried to the stable behind the house. She swiftly put a bridle on her father's horse, which was used both for riding and for pulling the buggy. She mounted bareback and rode him out through the stable door.

Down into the bed of Conejos Creek she went, turning immediately away from town. She kicked the horse in the ribs with her heels and he broke into a lope.

The sun was low in the west. There weren't more

73

than a couple of hours of sunlight left. By the time her father discovered she was gone, by the time he realized she had taken the horse, it would be too late for trailing her. And by morning she could be far away.

Her biggest regret now was that she had lacked the courage to kill herself. But maybe by running away, by removing herself from her parents' life, she could make amends.

For a while after riding the buggy horse down into the creekbed, Susan just let him go, neither urging him on nor holding him back. The placid animal maintained a walk for several miles before, sensing the lack of guidance from his rider he stopped, lowered his head and began to graze.

For a long time Susan sat on his back, numb and stunned. The enormity of what she had done overwhelmed her and made rational thought impossible. Her lie had caused the death of poor, simple-minded Billy Pinto, who had never hurt anything or anybody in his life. It had made a murderer out of her father and had made murderers out of five of his friends.

She couldn't see how she could make amends. She had tried taking her own life but had failed because of her lack of courage. Now she was running away, but if she did not display more courage than she had before, she would also fail in that.

And she wasn't courageous. She was cowardly or she wouldn't have lied last night. Suddenly she became aware that the sun was down, that most of the

74

light had faded from the sky. It was rapidly getting dark. She didn't know where the time had gone.

Where could she go, she asked herself. How could she live? This was Arizona Territory, Apacheland. What if the Apaches learned of Billy Pinto's death and came looking for her? A chill of terror ran down her spine. She had heard what Apaches did to the whites they captured. A lot of the whispered talk at school had dealt with the things they did to the women and girls they captured before death mercifully rescued the victims from their miseries.

The sky was, by now, nearly dark. The horse raised his head and stared at something in the darkness, ears pricked forward.

For several moments, Susan sat as if frozen on the horse's back, scarcely daring to breathe. She heard rustling in the grass from the direction in which the horse was looking.

In her terror she did not remember that it had been several years since the last Apache had left the reservation. Guilt over Billy Pinto's death had her in its grip. In Susan's mind, only cruel-faced Apaches could be there in the darkness, creeping closer, rustling the grass. They would seize her, strip her, stake her out. . . .

With a scream frozen in her throat, choking her, she slid from the horse's back. Blindly she fled into the darkness.

A tree branch, lying dry and dead on the ground, tripped her up. In her mind it was an Indian, clawing her, tearing at her clothes. Frantic and hysterical, she fought free of it, struggled to her feet and fled again. She crashed head-on into a tree. Her face struck its trunk first and she thought the blow came from an Apache's fist. She crumpled at the base of the tree, begging incoherently for her life.

The sounds she made frightened the buggy horse and he snorted with his fear. That sound became to Susan the snorting of Apache ponies and she struggled to her feet and ran again.

Tripped up often by her skirts, falling, rising, falling, she ran until she could run no more. With nothing to run from and nothing to run toward, she traveled in a rough circle less than three hundred yards in diameter so that when she finally collapsed and lost conscious-ness, she was still less than two hundred yards from her nervous and frightened horse. She appeared to be asleep, or dead, but her guilt still gave her no peace. Nightmares tormented her. Her body twitched and jerked, and later, in the cold, trembled violently. She was still less than five miles from her father's house.

It was a long time before Ben Hurd was able to con-trol himself. When he realized fully that he had been sobbing like a baby in his wife's arms, he pulled away, embarrassed and ashamed. With the roughness of a sleeve, he wiped his eyes, turning his face away so that he wouldn't have to look at his wife. He growled, "I've got to get back to the store."

"What are you going to do?"

He couldn't tell her he was planning another murder

to save himself from the consequences of the first. So he mumbled, "I don't know. I guess I'll have to try and figure something out."

She was silent. She might have told him not to worry but the admonition would have been meaningless. Nearly anything she could say would be meaningless.

He went out through the kitchen. Outside, he realized that his eyes and face were probably red and would give him away. So he slid down the path into the bed of Conejos Creek and began aimlessly to walk. He walked toward the bridge but when he realized doing so would put him within sight of the gallows, he turned the other way.

He walked for ten or fifteen minutes. Then, having calmed as much as he thought he was likely to, and having decided the telltale redness was gone from his eyes and face, he climbed out of the creekbed and headed for the store. Maybe if he busied himself with work, hard work, he would be able to better tolerate what was happening to him. At least it was worth a try.

An hour before sundown, a tall, gaunt man of about forty-five rode into town across the old wooden Conejos Creek bridge. He was stopped briefly to stare at the gallows and the ramshackle building that had once been the stage depot. His horse's hoofs clattered on the bridge, then were deadened by the deep dust of Graneros Avenue.

He stopped in front of the jail, dismounted and tied, then went to the door over which a sign reading *Sheriff* hung. He opened it and stepped inside.

Thorpe Stedman glanced up. The gaunt man crossed the room and stuck out his hand. "I'm Rufus Bell. The Indian agent wired that you wanted a U.S. marshal here."

Thorpe Stedman got up and took the hand. "I'm Thorpe Stedman. An Indian was lynched here last night while I was out of town. I figured him being an Indian meant that federal authorities were supposed to be in on it. Besides, I think I'm going to need some help."

Bell shoved his hat back and wiped his forehead with the back of his hand. Stedman got up. "Sit down here. You look tired. You must've made pretty good time to get here so soon."

Bell sank into the swivel chair. He put his dirty boots up on the desk. "I just happened to be in Raymer, thirty miles east of here. But I've been riding most of the day. Mind laying it out for me?"

Stedman told him about returning to town last night and finding the body of Billy Pinto hanging from the gallows on the other side of Conejos Creek. He told him about reading sign at the site this morning, and about trailing and catching up with Hughie Diggs. He nodded toward the back of the room. "I've got him back there for safekeeping now."

"How many men were involved?"

"Six. I think I know three of them but so far I

haven't been able to get Hughie Diggs to talk. He's too damn scared and he thinks if he keeps still that he'll be safe."

"Like hell he will. He'd be safer if he'd give you all six names."

Stedman then told him about his suspicions that Susan Hurd had been involved and about the confrontation a little while ago between himself and Hurd. He showed Bell his tongue, grinning ruefully. "He hit me in the mouth so hard I damn near bit off my tongue. I won't be able to touch a cup of coffee for a week."

"Where's Hurd now?"

"He stomped away toward home. I expect by now he's gotten the truth out of his daughter. He knows he and the others hanged the wrong man."

The marshal nodded and got up from the swivel chair. He said, "I'm going to stable my horse and get myself a room. If you need me I'll be at the hotel."

Stedman shook his hand a second time. Bell's grip was firm without being overly so. Stedman thought that a man's handshake told you a lot about him in just an instant of time. This one was competent and sure of himself and he didn't have anything to prove. He discovered that he liked Bell and that was going to make things easier.

Bell went out the door, untied his horse, mounted, and headed for the livery barn. Stedman went out back to talk to Hughie Diggs, to try once more to get the six names out of him.

He thought of Serena. He hoped all this would be over soon so that they could be married and go away. He could hire a deputy to take over for him for a couple of weeks. Excitement touched him, then went away as he began to talk to Hughie Diggs, sitting miserable and confused on the cot in his cell.

## Chapter 9

At six-thirty, Hurd locked up the store, said good night to his clerk, Mrs. Brackett, and headed home. He dreaded it. He dreaded facing his wife and he didn't even want to see Susan at all. He dreaded the meeting with the other five that was scheduled for eight-thirty that night. He had worked hard for the last couple of hours, restocking shelves, doing the heaviest work he could find. He'd gotten himself dusty and sweaty but it hadn't changed anything. He still faced the consequences of what he had done last night. He still knew he had murdered an innocent man, [even if that man was only an Indian]. He still faced the impending ruin of his life.

His anger was gone now, replaced by the most terrible depression he had ever experienced. He walked heavily, woodenly.

His wife's face was streaked with tears and her eyes were red from weeping. Susan was nowhere to be seen. Hurd asked, "Where is she, still up in her room?"

"I suppose so. I haven't heard a sound out of her."

Hurd knew he ought to go up. He'd pretty much laid blame for the whole thing on Susan but it wasn't entirely her fault. It was true that her actions and her lie had precipitated things. But he hadn't had to hang Billy Pinto for what he thought he'd done. He could have waited until the sheriff returned. He could even have locked Billy Pinto in the jail himself.

Had Susan accused a white boy, or man, that probably was what he would have done, he admitted reluctantly. He might have thrashed the man to vent his fury, but it was extremely doubtful if he'd have hanged him. Nor would the other five men have gone along with a lynching if the accused had been a white.

He climbed the stairs heavily, noticing that the door to his own and his wife's bedroom was ajar. He went down the hall to close it, out of curiosity peering in. He saw the shotgun on the bed. He picked it up, eased the hammers down, and unloaded it.

He was instantly overcome with compassion for Susan because it was obvious that she had considered taking her own life. It was also obvious that she hadn't been able to summon up the nerve.

He went down the hall to the door of Susan's room. He knocked, then opened the door and stepped inside.

Susan was gone. The window stood open, the curtains blowing slightly in the breeze. Worried now, Hurd ran down the stairs. He ran through the kitchen and out to the stable. He looked in and saw that the horse was gone.

Hurd had never, in his whole life, had occasion to try trailing anyone although he would have tried this morning, along with Steiner and Henshaw, to trail Hughie Diggs if they hadn't run into the sheriff first. Now he studied the ground, able to pick out the prints of Susan's small feet in the dust, the hoofprints of the horse as it was ridden out through the door. Walking slowly, he followed the prints to the cutbank path that led down into the bed of Conejos Creek.

He stopped here and glanced at the sky. The sun was down, with its fading rays staining a few high, thin clouds. Hurd knew that all he could hope to do, all anybody could hope to do, would be to ascertain which direction Susan had gone. In ten minutes it would be too dark to trail.

His wife had come out of the house. Now she called querulously, "Ben? Ben? Is something the matter? Where's Susan, Ben?"

He didn't bother to answer her. He hurried down the path, following the horse's prints which were hard to separate, now, from other horse prints and from the hoofprints of the cow.

At the bottom of the path he cast back and forth in ever-widening semicircles until he finally found what he thought were the freshest prints. The horse had headed west, away from town.

He followed along for a couple of hundred yards, satisfying himself. By the time he turned back, all light had died from the clouds and the sky was gray.

His wife stood at the head of the path. Hurd said,

"Susan's gone. She went out her window and took the horse. God knows how long she's been gone."

"Maybe she just went after the cow."

"Huh uh. She walks to get the cow."

"Where could she have gone?"

"God only knows. One thing I'm thankful for—there aren't any Apaches running loose."

"Maybe she didn't go very far. Maybe she's somewhere in town. Hadn't we better search and find out?"

Hurd nodded. He hadn't thought of that. Susan had tried to kill herself and had lacked the nerve. Maybe she had also lacked the nerve to leave town. He started away toward town, only to have his wife say, "It won't hurt to take time to eat. It's all ready and if she's in town nothing's going to happen to her. She's probably with one of her friends."

Hurd started toward the house. He heard the cowbell and saw the cow walking slowly along the bed of the creek. He got a bucket from the back porch and went to the stable. The cow came in and he gave her some grain while he sat down on the stool to milk. Finished, he shut the cow in and carried the milk to the house.

Supper was on the table. He ate quickly, woodenly, not because he was hungry but because he knew he needed all the strength that he could get. He was meeting the other five who had participated in the lynching last night at eight-thirty at his store. He could get them to help him search the town for Susan. They'd probably find her. They had to find her. He caught himself feeling frantic at the thought that something might be happening to her.

If it did, he'd be to blame. He'd laid too much of what had happened on Susan's shoulders. He thought of her standing up there in the bedroom trying to get up the nerve to kill herself and he felt his throat close up. His wife asked, "Ben, what's the matter? Do you think something has happened to her?"

He shook his head. "No. She's probably all right. As soon as I finish here I'll get somebody to help me and we'll search the town."

"What if you don't find her?"

"Then we'll get up a search party tomorrow and follow her trail. Nothing's going to happen to her. It's only September and one night in the open isn't going to hurt her much."

He left the house and hurried through the dusk to his store. He unlocked it and went in. He lighted a single lamp. It seemed as though it ought to be later than it was but the clock said eight.

Fifteen minutes later Henshaw came in followed by Steiner. Peter Judd came next, with Martin Watts, the town carpenter, right behind. Curtis Redding was last, his face looking as though he had decided not to come at all but had, at the last minute, changed his mind.

Hurd closed the door and drew the blinds. He said, "Before we worry about Hughie Diggs, I've got to ask your help. Susan's gone. We had an awful row this afternoon and she took the horse and left."

Henshaw asked, "Row? What about?"

Hurd hesitated. He hadn't realized that if he told

these men about the row with Susan he'd also have to tell them the cause of it. He said lamely, trying to avoid the truth, "One of those family things. You know. But I'd appreciate it if you'd all help me look for her. She's got to be in town someplace."

Redding said, "Wait a minute. If she's in town why are you so worried about her? She's sixteen years old and it isn't even nine yet."

Hurd groped frantically for an answer. Finally he said, "It was that thing last night. She's upset. You can understand that."

"But why did you have such a fight with her if she's so upset? I've got a feeling you're not telling us everything."

Hurd glared at him truculently. "If you don't want to help, the hell with you!"

Redding shrugged. "Hell, I'll help. I'd just like to know what's going on."

Hurd, relieved, said, "Then let's get at it." The other five would learn, eventually, that they'd hanged the wrong man. Stedman knew it and Stedman would tell them. But he didn't want them to know now because if they found out now they wouldn't help him hunt for Susan.

The five went out. Hurd directed them to reach different sectors of the town. He himself headed for the homes of Susan's friends, where she would most likely be.

House after house he visited, without success. It was now pitch dark. A thin overcast kept even the stars from shining through. At Rachel Borgman's house he was told, "Maybe she's with Mark."

"Mark Rulison?"

"Uh huh. They've been seeing each other some. I wasn't supposed to tell but I guess I'd better now."

Hurd headed for the Rulison house, which stood on the edge of town at E and First. He felt encouraged for the first time. Susan probably was there. And everything was going to be all right. He'd find her and take her home and then, later tonight, he and the others would do something about Hughie Diggs. Without a witness against them, there wouldn't be a damned thing Sheriff Stedman could do.

The Rulison house was a two-story frame, one of the older houses in the town. There was a lamp burning in the kitchen. Ben Hurd knocked.

Mark Rulison came to the door. He stared with shocked surprise at Hurd. He whirled, as if to run back into the house, but Hurd grabbed him by his shirt. "She's here, isn't she?"

Mark's face had gone dead white. His eyes looked like those of a cornered animal. He began to shake violently. He choked, and finally got out the words, "No, sir. She ain't here!"

Mrs. Rulison came to the door behind him. "What's going on out here?"

Hurd did not release the boy, a tall, gangling youngster the same age as Susan was. He said, "I'm looking for Susan. Is she here?"

"No, she ain't here. Why should she be?"

Hurd looked back at Mark. If Susan wasn't here, why was Mark so terrified? There could be only one reason and he knew what it was. Mark was the one who had been with Susan last night. He was the one who had fled and left her to face the consequences alone. His flight had been the cause of Susan's lie and of the hanging that had followed it.

Backing away, he yanked Mark along with him. Half a dozen feet from the back door, he drew back his fist and smashed Mark Rulison squarely in the face.

Mark stumbled backward, his shirt tearing, leaving a handful of it in Ben Hurd's grasp. Hurd was after him like a wolf.

Mrs. Rulison screamed. She seized a broom leaning against the porch wall beside the door and rushed at Hurd. She began belaboring him over the head and shoulders with the broom.

Hurd was astride Mark now, beating his head against the ground. "It was you, wasn't it?" he roared. "It was you with Susan last night! And you ran away. You chicken-livered little bastard, you ran away!"

Mrs. Rulison was screaming frantically at Hurd, wanting to know what this was all about. He turned his head to answer her and got the broom squarely in the face. There was the sound of voices shouting and the sound of running feet, and suddenly hands were pulling Ben Hurd away.

Stedman was the last to arrive, mounted and therefore less short of breath than the others were. Ben Hurd stood apart, disheveled and dusty, facing the bloody, terrified boy. Mrs. Rulison looked up at Stedman. "Sheriff, arrest this man!" she shrilled. "He came here and attacked my son for no reason at all! He's a crazy man, that's what he is!"

Stedman looked at Mark. "So you're the one?"

Mrs. Rulison screamed, "The one what? What is this all about?"

Stedman said, "Mr. Hurd caught someone with his daughter last night. The boy ran away. Susan accused Billy Pinto and told her father it was rape."

A man's voice whispered in shocked horror, "Holy Jesus Christ!"

Mrs. Rulison's face had lost its flush. She was, for the moment, speechless. Finally she managed to say, "That Indian was hanged because of what Susan accused him of?"

Stedman said, "Yes, ma'am."

She looked at her son. "And if you'd stayed—if you stood up and taken the blame like a man, he wouldn't have been hanged."

Mark Rulison didn't answer her. He was scared but there was sullenness in him too. Suddenly she swung the flat of her hand. It connected solidly with the side of her son's face.

Stedman said, "All right, go on home, all of you."

People began to drift away. Mrs. Rulison herded Mark back into the house threatening him with the broom. Stedman rode back toward the jail.

He had been watching faces in that crowd back there. The one who had been so terribly shocked had been the printer, Curtis Redding. But there had been other shocked expressions in that group, so that didn't necessarily prove anything. At least it proved nothing that would hold up in court.

# Chapter 10

Thorpe Stedman, who had gotten Hughie Diggs his supper before being drawn to the Rulison house by Mrs. Rulison's shrill screaming, now got the empty tray and carried it back to the restaurant, taking care to lock the jail door before leaving it. When he returned, the telegrapher, Sam Leonard, was waiting for him. Stedman took the telegram, glancing at Leonard's face as he did. Leonard's expression was both worried and scared.

Stedman went in, lighted the lamp, and slid the telegram out of the envelope. It was from the Indian agent on the Apache reservation. It read, GREGORIO HAS LEFT RESERVATION TAKING SEVEN OTHERS AND THEIR FAMILIES. BILLY PINTO NEPHEW OF GREGORIO. AFRAID HE INTENDS TO USE PINTO'S DEATH AS EXCUSE FOR MAKING WAR. SUGGEST YOU WARN RANCHERS AND SETTLERS SOONEST POSSIBLE. It was signed, THOMAS HAAS, AGENT.

Stedman sat down in his swivel chair. He read the telegram again. How in the hell could Gregorio have heard about Billy Pinto's death? Well, there was one way he could have learned. Some English-speaking Indian could have been hanging around the telegraph office when his telegram arrived notifying the agent of Billy Pinto's death. Whoever it was could have told Gregorio and everyone else who would listen. Now there was going to be hell to pay.

It was possible, of course, that Gregorio wouldn't come this way. If he was only using Pinto's death as an excuse, he might head south into Mexico and the Sierra Madre, long an Apache stronghold. But Stedman knew he didn't dare count on it. Gregorio, being related to Billy Pinto, might come straight here and try to exact revenge for Billy's death.

Stedman knew Gregorio by sight. The Apache was about forty, squat, bowlegged and as fierce as a bobcat. He had been with Geronimo on several of his forays but he had never been caught. The last time, when Geronimo had finally been forced to surrender, Gregorio had been sick with smallpox and had therefore not been with him. His face was now a mass of smallpox scars, which did not make him any handsomer.

Bell came in, idly picking his teeth. Stedman handed him the telegram. Bell read it and whistled. His face wasn't scared but it was grave. "That's all this country needs right now, another Apache outbreak. I know Gregorio. He don't give a damn about Billy Pinto or how he died. All this just gives him a chance to murder some more whites."

Stedman shrugged. "It doesn't matter what his reasons are. He's just as dangerous either way."

"What about the Army? The agent didn't say anything about letting them know."

Stedman grunted disgustedly. "You know how long it will take them to move. Gregorio will have done his damage and be a hundred miles away before they put a trooper into the field."

Bell grinned faintly. "Then it's up to me and you."

Stedman nodded. He said, "Gregorio speaks and understands English as good as you and me. Maybe if we had the men who hanged Billy Pinto in jail, he'd back off without killing anyone."

"Maybe. But how are you going to manage it?"

"Get Hughie Diggs to talk. First, though, I'm going to get myself something to eat. Will you hold this place down while I'm gone?"

"Sure." The marshal took Stedman's chair when Stedman rose. The sheriff put on his hat and went out the door. He walked along the dark street to the restaurant. There seemed to be neither more nor fewer people on the street than usual.

He wondered when Gregorio had left the reservation. Probably before dark or else the agent wouldn't have known that he was gone. Which meant that the Apaches could be outside Graneros by dawn or sooner. Waiting. Looking for victims, innocent or otherwise.

He ordered the stew because he knew it was ready and would be served immediately. He ate as quickly as he could, short of gulping down his food. He was still appalled and horrified at the amount of damage done by one girl's lie. And it wasn't over yet.

He finished eating, paid for his meal, and went outside. Somehow he had to get those six names out of Hughie Diggs, which meant he had to convince Hughie it was less dangerous for him to tell than it was to remain silent. He walked back to the jail.

He went in and bolted the door behind him. He picked up the lamp and headed for the door leading to the cells. Reaching it, he handed the lamp to Bell, who had followed him.

He opened the door. There was a corridor about twenty feet long leading between the two rows of cells to the stone back wall. There were three cells to a side, making a total of six in all, each eight by seven feet.

Hughie Diggs sat on his cot in the first cell on the right, blinking at the light. He had been in total darkness and had apparently been lying down. Stedman led the way to his cell door. Bell held the lamp high, peering through the bars at Hughie.

Suddenly, Stedman's eye caught a movement on the other side of the room. He snatched his gun from its holster, raised it, and thumbed back the hammer simultaneously. Poking between the bars was the steel muzzle of a rifle. As his gun came up, he roared, "Hughie! Hit the floor!"

All was confusion for a moment. He let his shot go and heard the bullet ricochet away into the night sky as it struck the stone window frame and glanced off. The rifle in the cell window flared and at the same instant Bell slammed the lamp down to the floor. It had no more than struck before Bell had whirled and leaped through the door into the office. He reached the outside door, fumbled an instant for the bolt, then flung open the door and plunged outside.

Stedman, smoking gun in hand, tried hard to see into Hughie's cell. The smell of kerosene from the smashed lamp was overpowering and the glass from the shattered lamp chimney grated beneath his feet. He asked, "Hughie? You all right?"

He heard movement in Hughie's cell. Damn it, he though, they've shot him after I promised that he'd be safe. He repeated, "Hughie? You all right?"

Hughie's voice was thin and scared. "Yes, sir. I'm all right."

"You're not hit? You're sure?"

"No, sir. I'm all right."

Bell returned, closing and bolting the outside door. He said, "Nobody in sight. There was a ladder standing against the wall. I smashed it."

Enough light came from the office and fell into the cell corridor for Stedman to clean up the shattered lamp. He swept up the broken glass and dumped it into a box kept in the corner for trash. Bell said, "You'd better get that boy to talk."

Stedman nodded. Someone was knocking on the office door. He nodded at Bell, silently telling him to cover the door, then slid back the bolt and opened it. Jesse Durham, the county clerk, stood outside, hatless and looking scared. Some other people stood beyond

93

in the darkness, watching. Durham said, "I heard shots. Is everything all right?"

Stedman nodded.

"What happened?"

"Somebody tried to kill Hughie Diggs. Do something for me, will you, Jesse? Find Martin Watts and ask him to bring some lumber and tools down here. I want the jail windows boarded up so nobody can see in."

"Sure. I'll get him right away." Durham hurried away. Stedman guessed he had been working late in the courthouse next door, which explained how he had heard the shots. He wondered briefly if Durham could be one of those he was seeking, then decided he probably was not. If he had been, he wouldn't call attention to himself unnecessarily.

"You going to talk to Diggs?" asked Bell.

"Uh huh. But let's wait until those windows are boarded up. He'll feel safer then."

"How many names do you already know?"

"I think I know three of them. Early this morning, when I was starting out to trail Hughie Diggs, I ran into three men with rifles heading the same way I was."

"What were their names?"

"Ben Hurd, Rufus Henshaw and Max Steiner."

"You could jail them on suspicion."

"I thought of it. But three of them would still be loose. I'd just as soon get them all at once."

"I hope we get it nailed down before the newspapers

in Tucson get hold of it."

"So do I." Stedman could visualize this little town with newspaper reporters swarming over everything. Nervously, he began pacing back and forth. Bell watched him silently.

Half an hour passed. Finally there was a knock on the door. Opening it, Stedman saw Martin Watts outside. He was carrying his toolbox and had on overalls. Behind him were his two sons, Freddie and John, each carrying an armload of used pine boards.

Stedman held the door and the three filed in. Watts opened the door leading to the cells. Stedman followed, carrying the lamp.

From Hughie Diggs he heard a gasp of indrawn breath. He glanced that way and saw Hughie staring at Martin Watts, pure terror in his eyes.

So now he knew the fourth. Martin Watts. Watts took pains not to even glance at Hughie Diggs. Using his two sons for helpers, he went to the last two unlocked cells and started work. Stedman stood in the doorway, watching.

Only two of the cells had windows, the two farthest to the rear. It took Watts less than half an hour to board them up. He drove wedges between the boards and the stone window frames to hold the boards in place. Stedman watched this operation carefully. He didn't want anybody pushing the boards away and taking a pot shot at Hughie Diggs again.

When he was finished, Watts gathered up his tools and left. Stedman got the broom and swept up the sawdust and scraps. When he had finished, he unlocked Hughie's cell and went in. He sat down beside Hughie on the cot. "There. It's all done. Nobody can hurt you now."

Hughie looked at him gratefully. "Thanks, Mr. Stedman."

"You can tell me who those six men were. I can get them in jail and then I can let you go."

The grateful look vanished from Hughie's face. His eyes turned scared again and Stedman realized he was thinking about how close Martin Watts had been to him only a few moments before. He said, "Hughie, I can't put them in jail unless you tell me who they are. I know four of them already but I haven't any proof. If I brought them into court, the judge would let them go. And as long as they're loose, you're in danger. Can't you see that?"

Stubbornly Hughie said, "I don't know nothing, Mr. Stedman. I didn't see nobody."

Stedman shrugged. He got up. "Want a lamp back here?"

"No, sir. I feel better in the dark."

"All right, Hughie." Stedman took the lamp and returned to the office after locking the door of Hughie's cell. He hated keeping Hughie in jail but turning him loose would be like throwing him to the wolves.

Suddenly he heard a shout out in the street. It was followed by other shouts. He hurried to the door, slid back the bolt, and opened it.

The street was lighted by an orange glow. Looking down the street, Stedman saw a fire on the other side of Conejos Creek. The ruins of the old stage depot were in flames. So was the gallows standing in front of it.

## Chapter 11

Bell came into the street behind Stedman. Nobody seemed much concerned about the fire. Nobody rang the fire bell. Most of the townspeople were probably relieved to see the gallows being consumed.

Bell came out to stand beside Stedman. "Who do you reckon started that?"

"Somebody that was in on the hanging last night, I suppose. Somebody that couldn't stand to look at it any more."

He glanced up Graneros Avenue. In front of the Red Dog Saloon there must have been at least a dozen men. There were a handful in front of the hotel. There were a few others that had come from their homes or who had been on their way to or from someplace.

The old stage station itself was now completely ablaze, sending a column of flame fifty feet into the air. The gallows, slower to catch, had outlined itself in fire, but, being of heavy timbers, the flames consuming it were bluer and not as bright. It probably would never be completely consumed, thought

Stedman, and would remain standing in the morning, black and gaunt. It would have to be pulled down and destroyed. But then it should have been destroyed a long time ago.

He was turning away to go back inside the jail when his eye caught movement between the fire and the town. Horses. A lot of them. And riders, although silhouetted and in poor light it was hard to tell who or what they were.

Even yet, no alarm touched Stedman's mind. He stood there watching while the horsemen thundered across the bridge and up Graneros Avenue. He muttered, "What the hell is going on?"

The riders were now less than a block away. And with sudden shock, Stedman realized who they were. They were Indians. They were Gregorio and his malcontents. He roared, "Take cover! Take cover! It's Indians!" even as the first shots racketed.

Flashes came from rifle muzzles among the wildly galloping horsemen. Their shrill, yipping, terrifying cries mingled with the reports of their guns. The thunder of their horses' hoofs rumbled along the street and behind them, nearly obliterating the light from the fire, dust raised in a blinding cloud.

For too long the townspeople stood there, stunned, unbelieving. During all the Apache troubles never once had Indians dared to raid a town. To most it must have seemed like some kind of prank, perpetrated by cowboys from neighboring ranches. But Stedman knew it was no prank. He knew, if the town did not, of

98

Gregorio's leaving the reservation. He knew these were real Indians, bent on murder and not caring whether the guilty were the ones to die or the innocent.

He roared again, "Take cover! It's Indians!" There was no time now for diving into the sheriff's office, for seizing and loading a rifle or shotgun. The revolver in the holster at his side would have to do.

He backed against the building wall. He brought up his revolver, holding it solidly in both hands and thumbed the hammer back. He cursed the dust cloud rising behind the Indians because it cut the amount of light available.

Beside him, Bell was holding his own revolver similarly. Stedman was the first to fire, aiming at a horse instead of at a man because there was a better chance of scoring a hit. The horse at which he had been aiming dropped to his knees and somersaulted in the dusty street. His rider quit the horse the instant he started down and hit the ground running. He vaulted up behind one of his companions, that man's horse hardly breaking stride.

Bell was shooting now, methodically, carefully. And the Indians were firing, at people standing too stunned to move, at others scrambling for the nearest cover available.

Up toward the saloon a man yelled with pain as he was hit. Stedman continued firing regularly and methodically but the first of the Indians had by now thundered past and shooting was made more difficult by dust. Stedman thought he hit one because he saw the man flinch and sway, but the Indian and his horse went on to be lost in the cloud of dust.

It was over as suddenly as it had begun. Dust lay in the street like a pall. The horse Stedman had downed lay in the middle of Graneros Avenue, kicking. Women were screaming up at the hotel. A few men were firing blindly and futilely into the darkness where the Indians had disappeared.

Slowly the dust cloud dissipated. Once more the street was lighted by the flames at the stage depot. A man's voice yelled, "Doc! Somebody get Doc Ross."

Doc Ross, as he was called, was no doctor at all. He was the town barber. He pulled teeth. He doctored sick horses and cows. And when there was need for it, he did his best for humans too.

Stedman and Bell walked up the street toward the hotel. The Indian horse had stopped kicking now, so there would be no need for shooting him.

Nearing Hurd's store, Stedman could hear a man groaning. He got closer and saw that it was Max Steiner, who lay flat on his back on the narrow boardwalk. Men crowded around him, staring down. Doc Ross arrived at the same time Stedman did and pushed them angrily away. "For God's sake, give the man some air! Get away from him!"

Steiner's glance met Stedman's and clung to it. He was pale and when Ross tried to peel his clothing away from the wound, his face contorted with the pain. The wound was in his chest and there was a light froth of blood coming from the wound and also from his mouth.

He said, "He knew, didn't he? He got me because I helped kill Billy Pinto."

Stedman didn't say anything. He hadn't thought anybody in town knew about Gregorio leaving the reservation but apparently he'd been wrong. Sam Leonard must have blabbed it all over town.

He shook his head, rejecting in his mind the temptation to ask Steiner who the others were who had hanged Billy Pinto. Steiner was dying. Nobody could live with a bullet through his lungs. Not for very long. Stedman said, "They'd have had no way of knowing you were in on that. Even if they had, it would have been too dark to pick you out. You just happened to get it, that's all."

Steiner accepted that. The look in his eyes told Stedman he also accepted something else—that this was the retribution of the Lord. Doc Ross glanced up at Stedman and almost imperceptibly shook his head. Steiner's eyes were closed now. His breathing was labored. And then he simply stopped breathing altogether.

Stedman quieted his vague feeling of guilt over his failure to ask Steiner for the others' names by telling himself Steiner wouldn't have had time anyway. Which was true. He said, "Get Dallas Wagoner to come get his body."

He faced the little crowd. He yelled, "Go home. Arm yourselves and keep your guns handy. If they come

101

back, I'll see that the courthouse bell wakes you up."

Nobody asked questions, which told him, if Steiner's words had not, that Sam Leonard had blabbed about the breakout all over town. He spotted Sam Leonard at the edge of the crowd and collared him as Sam was hurrying away. He said, "I ought to let the company know how confidential the telegrams are that come through here."

Leonard didn't say anything but he tried to pull away. Stedman said, "You take the first watch at the courthouse. If the Indians come back, ring the bell."

"All right, Sheriff."

"And stay awake. If you go to sleep on the job, I promise you I'll let your company know what a big mouth you've got."

Leonard hurried away. As an afterthought, Stedman broke into a run and caught up with him. "Before you go up in the bell tower, I've got a telegram I want you to send."

He followed Leonard to the telegraph office. It was never kept open at night because there weren't enough messages coming into Graneros to justify it. Leonard unlocked the door and lighted the lamp. Stedman got a blank and scrawled out a message addressed to the Commandant at Fort Curry, sixty miles to the east. He didn't think it was going to do any good to ask for help but he didn't want anyone saying he hadn't done all he should. The message said, "GREGORIO OFF RESERVATION WITH SIX OR EIGHT FOL- LOWERS. ATTACKED GRANEROS TONIGHT.

REQUEST CAVALRY TROOP IMMEDIATELY. He signed his name and underneath it wrote, SHERIFF, CONEJOS COUNTY, ARIZONA.

Leonard busied himself at the telegraph key. He finished, waited and the instrument chattered an acknowledgment. Stedman said dryly, "If you can find anybody still up, you can tell them the cavalry is on the way."

Leonard flushed. He blew out the lamp and followed Stedman out the door. He went to the courthouse and climbed the outside stairway to the bell cupola.

Stedman went to the jail. Bell was waiting in the doorway. "Send for the troops?"

"Uh huh. They're sixty miles away, though, and they won't start until morning even if they start then. It'll be late tomorrow evening before they can get here."

"What are you going to do about that horse?"

"Leave him there. I'll get somebody to drag him away in the morning."

The street was deserted now. The fire down at the old stage station had about burned itself out. The gallows fire had gone out except for some smoldering spots that glowed when fanned by the breeze.

Stedman went into the jail. Bell followed and Stedman bolted the door. Bell said, "This is a lot of trouble over one girl's lie."

"It sure as hell is. And it's about time we put a stop to it. It's about time that damn Hughie Diggs did some talking, too."

103

He picked up a lamp and carried it through the door leading to the cells. He unlocked Hughie's cell and carried the lamp inside. There was a low stool and he put the lamp down on that.

Standing, looking down at Hughie, he asked, "Hear the commotion?"

"Yes, sir." Hughie's eyes were scared. Stedman felt a momentary pity. Hughie's life wasn't an easy one and after this was over it wasn't going to be any easier. The families of the men he named would make things just as hard for him as they could.

Stedman said, "That was Gregorio, raiding the town. Gregorio was related to Billy Pinto. He's using Billy's death as an excuse to start the Indian wars all over again."

Hughie's face was pale and he stared steadily at the floor between his feet. Stedman said, "You know what it's going to take to get Gregorio back on the reservation?"

"No, sir."

"It's going to take the arrest of every one of the men who helped hang Billy last night."

Still Hughie didn't say anything. He began twisting his hands together. His knees began to shake. Stedman said, "Max Steiner is dead, Hughie. One of Gregorio's Indians shot him in the chest."

Hughie looked up, his eyes filled with agony. "It ain't right to blame me for what's happenin'. I didn't have nothing to do with it."

"But you can put a stop to it. You know damned well

you can. And you're the only one who can."

Hughie's knees trembled more violently. Stedman said, "It won't matter to them whether you tell me or not. If you don't tell, they'll maybe be more anxious to kill you than if you do. They'll want you dead so that you can't ever tell."

Hughie's shoulders slumped. He looked up and there were tears now in his eyes. "All right, Mr. Stedman. I'll tell you who they were."

Stedman turned his head. Bell was standing just outside the cell. He said, "I want you to listen to this. I may need you as a witness in court."

Bell nodded. Stedman turned back to Hughie. "All right, Hughie, go ahead."

"Mr. Hurd was the one that was eggin' 'em on. He claimed Billy had hurt his daughter. But I know that ain't so, Mr. Stedman. Billy wouldn't hurt nobody. He never even looked at her."

Stedman said, "I know he didn't, Hughie. I know Billy didn't do anything wrong."

"Mr. Steiner was another. And there was Mr. Henshaw, and Mr. Watts, the one that was in here fixing the windows a while ago, and Mr. Redding and Mr. Judd."

The last name hit Stedman like a blow in the stomach. It had never even occurred to him that Serena's brother might have been one of those who had lynched the Indian. Almost numbly he asked, "Did you try to stop them, Hughie?"

"Yes, sir. At first I thought they was just tryin' to

scare Billy. They dragged him down the creek and up and across the bridge and I followed and stayed out of sight. When they got there, I hid in that old shack." His eyes were suddenly filled with suffering. "I didn't know they was really goin' to do it, Mr. Stedman. I swear I didn't. By the time I did know, it was too late. I ran out but Billy was already hanging there. That was when one of them started chasing me on the horse."

Stedman picked up the lamp. "All right, Hughie. You get some sleep. And don't be blaming yourself. There wouldn't have been anything you could have done, no matter what. They'd just have killed you too."

Hughie nodded. He seemed relieved to finally have the knowledge he had guarded so carefully off his chest.

Stedman locked him in. He carried the lamp back into the office. He was going to lose Serena over this. He could feel it in his bones. No matter what he did, he'd end up in the wrong. If he arrested Peter and threw him in jail with the others, she'd think he was persecuting him. And he had no other choice. No other choice at all.

He cursed sourly to himself. Serena shouldn't be forced into the position of having to make a choice between the two of them. Peter was her brother, the only blood relation she had in the world. She loved him despite his weaknesses. Maybe she loved him all the more because of his weakness and his dependence on her.

She'd never be able to turn her back on him, no matter what he did. Even if she believed him guilty she'd have to stand by him to the bitter end. It was doubtful if she'd be able to marry the man who arrested him, brought him to trial, and took him off to prison afterward.

Sick at heart, Stedman sat down in his swivel chair and stared blankly at the wall.

## Chapter 12

After the sheriff had left, and after Mrs. Rulison had herded her son back into the house, Ben Hurd just stood there, shattered, desolate, not knowing what to do next. People stared at him briefly the way they might have stared at some strange, unfamiliar kind of animal, then turned and faded away into the night. Two men remained, two of those who had helped Hurd lynch Billy Pinto the night before.

One of them, Curtis Redding, said in a horrified voice, "You were wrong! It wasn't even rape!"

Hurd didn't need Redding to tell him that. He'd been telling himself. But he also had been pushed nearly to his limit. His daughter had lied and gotten him into this. The boy had run away, causing her to lie. Now his daughter was gone and he faced prison or hanging for what he'd done. His life was in ruins. No matter what happened, it would never be the same again. The need to defend himself made him say defiantly, "Hell, he was only an Indian!"

Martin Watts said, "That ain't what the judge is going to say."

With horror in his voice Redding said, "Only an Indian? How can you say such a thing? He was a human being and he hadn't done anything!"

Hurd turned on him like a wolf. "You son-of-a-bitch! You helped! Don't you go getting so god-damned holy all of a sudden! You're just as guilty as any of us are."

Martin Watts wasn't as agitated as Hurd and Redding were. He said, "Standing here fighting about it ain't going to get us any place. Let's go on down to the store and meet just like we planned before Susan disappeared."

"What about the others? Henshaw, Steiner and Judd?"

"They'll come when they don't find the girl."

The three walked along the street to Ben Hurd's store. He unlocked the door and lighted a lamp. Sure enough, the other three showed up before five minutes had gone by. Hurd took the lamp and led them to the back room.

They were still arguing when Gregorio attacked the town. They blew out the lamp and streamed out the front door of the store to see what was going on. That was when Steiner got it in the chest.

The other five retreated instantly back into Hurd's darkened store. Hurd locked the door and the five groped their way to the back room. Not until that door had been securely fastened did Hurd again light a lamp.

The five were scared but they were also desperate. Each one of them knew that eventually Stedman was going to get their names out of Hughie Diggs if he had not already. Not a one of them could come up with a solution to the problem of what they were going to do. All five were afraid to venture out into the street, fearing that Stedman already knew their names and would arrest them as soon as they appeared. So they stayed in the back of Ben Hurd's store. He found a couple of bottles of whiskey and the five drank it gloomily. It made things no easier. Their dilemma did not go away.

Hurd fretted helplessly about where Susan was. He knew she was in mortal danger out there in the darkness with Gregorio and his followers on the loose. But there wasn't one damn thing he could do about it tonight. She couldn't be trailed until it got light tomorrow.

As soon as he had the names, Sheriff Thorpe Stedman left the jail. He heard Bell shoot the bolt behind him and knew that, with Bell on guard, Hughie Diggs would be all right until he got back.

He went to Ben Hurd's house first. As he had expected, Hurd wasn't home. Hurd's wife said he was probably still hunting Susan. She was almost beside herself with fear. She knew Gregorio was out in the darkness someplace with his followers and his hate. Her imagination wouldn't let her rest as she thought of

Susan falling into his hands.

Stedman tried to reassure her, without much success. He left and headed for the house of Martin Watts. Watts wasn't at home either. Nor was Curtis Redding in his room at the hotel.

Judd had a room above the saloon. There was no answer to the sheriff's knock and the door was locked. Stedman went to Henshaw's last, not at all surprised when Henshaw's wife said he was still out looking for Susan Hurd. Stedman didn't tell her differently.

The five had to be together, probably at Ben Hurd's store. He went there and found the front door locked. He went around to the alley and found the back door also locked.

He heard no sound but he felt sure the five were inside. Had he felt it was important enough, he might have gotten a posse together and forced the door. But he knew the five weren't going anywhere. They'd still be in town when the sun came up. And there was no chance of appeasing Gregorio with their arrests tonight if there ever had been a chance. Stedman believed Gregorio was just using the death of Billy Pinto as an excuse for killing whites. Next to Geronimo he probably hated them more bitterly than any other Apache alive.

He returned to the jail and Bell admitted him. Bell had made a fire in the stove and had brewed some fresh coffee. Stedman poured himself a cup and sat down in his swivel chair, which Bell obligingly vacated for him.

With a little luck, maybe he could get things nailed down tomorrow. He and Bell shouldn't have too much trouble finding and arresting the five men who had lynched Billy Pinto. He could organize a search party to hunt for Susan Hurd. He could station all the able-bodied men who were left along Graneros Avenue with rifles and shotguns. Gregorio might be fierce and tough but he was, after all, only a man.

But there'd be no sleep tonight. He didn't dare take the chance. He finished his coffee, had Bell let him out, then climbed the stairs to the courthouse bell cupola. Sam Leonard had a cigar going. Its fire made a comfortable glow in the darkness and the smoke was pleasantly fragrant. Stedman asked, "Can you stay awake or do you want to be relieved?"

"I can stay awake. It's kind of nice up here." He hesitated a moment and then he said, "I'm sorry about blabbing about Gregorio all over town."

Stedman shrugged. "No harm done, I guess. Don't let it worry you."

Staring down into the street from the height of the courthouse bell cupola, Stedman saw a man coming down the street from the direction of Ben Hurd's store. He hurried down the stairs and into the street in time to intercept the man in front of the jail.

It was Curtis Redding, the printer, very nervous and very agitated. He said breathlessly, "I've got to talk to you, Sheriff. I've got to talk to you right away."

"All right. Let's get in off the street."

Stedman knocked on the door and Bell unbolted it.

He and Redding went inside.

Redding's face was pale and his eyes were scared but there was a firm set of determination about his mouth. He said, "I can't keep it in any more, Sheriff. I've got to tell."

"All right, Mr. Redding. Sit down. Want some coffee?"

Redding sat down in a straight-backed chair. He shook his head to the offer of coffee. He blurted, "I was one of them, Sheriff. I helped to hang Billy Pinto last night."

Stedman nodded. "I know. I know all the names. I would like to know how it happened, though."

"Well, I was in my room at the hotel. Max Steiner came to my door. He said that Susan Hurd had been attacked and raped and that her father knew who it was. I said he'd better get you, but he said you were out of town. He asked me to help and I said I would." He glanced up at the sheriff, suddenly with a certain defensive quality in his eyes. "I thought it was my duty as a citizen, Sheriff. A crime had been committed, Steiner said he knew who it was, and you weren't here to handle it."

Stedman nodded. "Go on."

"Well, I went downstairs with Steiner. We met Hurd and the others up at Hurd's store. He told us what had happened. He was pretty upset, Sheriff. He said Susan had been raped by Billy Pinto and that Pinto had run away. He said Susan had told him who it was, and that he was going after Pinto and needed our help. Well, what could any man do, Sheriff? I didn't know what I was getting into and I doubt if the others did. If I thought about it at all, I probably assumed we were going to capture Pinto and put him in jail until you got back."

He stopped. His knees were shaking and so were his hands. His face had a pallor that was almost greenish. But there was a kind of self-punishing relief in his eyes as if he had wanted to get this off his chest ever since it had happened last night.

"The six of us got guns and went down to that little shack in the bed of Conejos Creek where Billy Pinto lives—lived. He was asleep. I guess we ought to have wondered about that. Someone who has just raped a girl wouldn't just go home and go to sleep. But Ben was all worked up. He attacked the Indian and started beating him and we had to pull him off. The Indian was scared—as scared as I've ever seen anyone. He kept spouting at us in Apache but none of us could understand any of it and the Indian seemed to have forgotten all the English he ever knew. If he ever knew very much. To tell you the truth, until last night I'd never ever heard his voice."

He looked at the coffeepot on the stove. "I'll have some coffee now, if you don't mind."

Stedman got him a cup and filled it with coffee from the pot. He handed it to Redding, who had to hold it with both hands to keep from spilling it. He gulped a couple of scalding swallows, then stared down at the shaking cup in his hands. "We dragged him out of there. We put a rope around his neck and dragged him to the bridge. Ben went to get a horse. He didn't say why and I didn't think to ask. When he came back we dragged the Indian across the bridge to the old stage depot. It was late and nobody was up. By this time Pinto wasn't saying anything or even making any sounds. The rope was tight around his neck and he was doing his best to keep it from choking him. Ben dragged him right over to that gallows and I started balking then and asking why we were taking him there. Ben said by God he wanted to throw a scare into him."

Stedman broke in, "Did you see Hughie Diggs?"

Redding shook his head. "None of us saw Hughie until he came out of the old stage station after . . . later on."

He gulped what remained of the coffee even though it still was scalding hot. He didn't seem to notice. He said, "I'm not trying to get out of it, Sheriff, but I swear to God that up until the last minute I thought we were just throwing a scare into him."

Stedman asked, "What about Judd? How did he get into it?"

"He heard us, I guess. I guess he heard the commotion and came to see what was going on. When he found out, he just went along with us."

Stedman looked at Bell, then back at Redding again. Redding said, "It was black as hell down where the gallows were. Ben got some dry sticks and built a little fire so we could see. He boosted the Indian up on the horse and he threw the rope over the gallows and tied it to one of the supports. That's when I started to protest, Sheriff. Both Steiner and I did. We told Ben this was going too far, and what if something happened to spook the horse. That's when Ben hit the horse on the rump with a board and the next minute the Indian was just hanging there. Hughie Diggs came running out and I started trying to untie the knot in the rope where Ben had tied it. I didn't have a knife. Things were all mixed up for a while and by the time I realized I couldn't untie the knot because of the weight of the Indian it was too late anyway. Somebody tried to catch Hughie Diggs, but he got away. I went off a ways and got sick. After that, I came back to the hotel."

Stedman took the empty cup out of Redding's shaking grasp. Redding got up. He said, "I'm ready now."

"Ready for what?"

"Ready to go to jail."

Stedman didn't think it was really necessary to lock Redding up, but he knew he might be criticized if he did not. He nodded and led the way to the cells at the rear. Bell held the lamp while Stedman unlocked a cell. Hughie stared at Redding with fear in his eyes.

The printer looked at him. "I'm sorry, Hughie. It's no excuse but until the last minute I thought they were only trying to throw a scare into him."

Hughie did not reply. Stedman and Bell left the

place in darkness and returned to the office. Stedman felt a little sick.

# Chapter 13

Watching from the darkened front window of his store, Ben Hurd saw the U.S. marshal, Bell, leave and walk to the hotel. He saw the lamp in the sheriff's office go out.

He called to the men in back, "It's all right now. The sheriff's gone to bed."

The men filed to the front of the store. Redding, when he had left earlier, had claimed to be going to the hotel but neither Hurd nor the others had believed him. They had watched while he walked down the street and then had seen him go into the sheriff's office. He had not reappeared, which meant he was locked up in jail. It also meant he had told the sheriff the whole story, and probably the names of the men who had taken part.

Hurd watched the others disappear into the darkness. Only four now were left. Steiner was dead. Redding was in jail.

Hurd didn't know what he was going to do tomorrow. It had to be faced, he knew that much. The penalty had to be paid. The hardest thing to face was the knowledge that he had been wrong. It had all been unnecessary. His life was ruined and so were the lives of the others and it was all for nothing, all because of a frightened young girl's stupid lie.

Wearily he locked the store and headed toward home. His mind was almost numb. Nothing could be changed. Billy Pinto was dead and he would have to pay for killing him.

What he must do now was try and pick up the pieces, insofar as that was possible, of his shattered life. Susan had run away and must be found before the Apaches happened onto her. There wasn't much danger of that tonight, Hurd thought, because she would have hidden herself and Gregorio and his fol- lowers had probably camped. In daylight, though, it would be different. She would be in great danger as soon as it got light. So would anybody out searching for her.

He doubted if anyone in town would help him look for her. Certainly the remaining three who had helped him hang Billy Pinto would not. Nor would anybody else. The whole town knew, by now, about the hanging. They knew it had been a mistake. They knew Gregorio was on the loose because of it.

The sheriff would help, he supposed, and so would the marshal, Bell. The trouble with asking them was the risk he'd take that they'd simply put him in jail. So he would have to go alone.

His wife was still up when he got home. A single lamp burned in the kitchen. She sat at the kitchen table, her eyes red from weeping, her face looking as if she had aged fifteen years in a single day and night. There was a question in her eyes that he understood.

He shook his head. "We didn't find her, and there were six men looking so I doubt if she's in town."

"Those Indians!" Her face was ghastly. "What if they find her?"

"They won't. They'd have no more chance of finding her in the dark than I would." He crossed the room, bent and kissed her forehead. "Don't you worry now. I'll go look for her as soon as it gets light enough to see the ground."

She nodded. They had been married almost eighteen years and she had great faith in him. He knew there were questions she wanted to ask. He knew she wanted to know all of it but he couldn't tell her all of it tonight. He picked up the lamp and headed upstairs and she meekly followed him.

He wondered how she and Susan would get along without him. He supposed the two of them could learn to run the store, but would the town forgive what he had done enough to patronize the store? He doubted it.

He told himself, as he undressed for bed, that he was too tired tonight to come to any intelligent decision. Tonight, he just felt like giving up, like doing what Redding had, confessing and letting himself be sent to prison. Tomorrow he'd probably feel differently. He'd feel like fighting for life and freedom.

He blew out the lamp and got into bed. He thought about Susan and knew his wife was thinking about her too. He remembered the shotgun, loaded and cocked, lying on the bed. His own remorse was terrible enough but Susan's must be twice as terrible because she knew it had all begun with her.

He lay awake for a long time. Finally exhaustion claimed him and he slept. He awakened while it was still dark. There was a line of gray along the horizon outside.

His wife was already up. She was downstairs in the kitchen, in nightgown and wrapper, fixing coffee and breakfast for him.

While she readied it, he went out, hurried to the livery stable, and saddled up a horse. He rode him home and tied him outside the kitchen door. He gulped two cups of coffee with his breakfast, which he didn't really want but which he knew he would need. By the time he had finished, the sky outside was turning gray.

He kissed his wife's pale lips. "It will be all right. You'll see, it will be all right."

She managed a wan smile. Hurd went out, untied and mounted, and rode down into the bed of Conejos Creek to where he had given up following Susan's trail yesterday. He had to wait several minutes before it was light enough to see the ground. Then he touched the horse's sides with his heels and began to follow Susan's trail.

It was easy, following, here in the bed of Conejos Creek. The ground was sandy and soft and the horse Susan was riding had left deep and plainly seen hoofprints.

Strangely enough, he didn't worry about being captured by Gregorio. In a way, he might even have welcomed it because it would have solved his problems, all of them, once and for all. He'd need make no more decisions. Everything would be decided for him. He realized, suddenly and with a shock, that he didn't even have a gun.

But he did not return for one. Eyes on the ground, he rode at a steady walk while the sky grew lighter. Eventually the sun came up.

Ben Hurd tried to think of someplace Susan might go, but he could think of none. Right now she was headed straight for the Apache reservation but that was twenty miles away and she could not possibly have gone that far last night.

Rounding a bend in the creekbed about five miles from town, he suddenly saw the horse standing in a little grove of scrub trees ahead of him. The horse's reins were trailing on the ground, but the animal was grazing despite the difficulty of chewing with the bit in his mouth. Ben kicked his livery stable horse into a trot.

Susan was sitting on the ground about fifty feet from the horse. Her face was streaked with tears and her thumb was in her mouth. She looked up at him without recognition but also without fear. He dismounted beside her. "Susan?"

Her eyes showed no recognition. He knelt in front of her and stared into her eyes. They were, in a way, like the eyes of a very young child, yet they did not even have the kind of comprehension you would expect from a child. They were more like the eyes of a young animal, faintly curious, unafraid but without comprehension or any memory of who she was, who he was, what had happened yesterday.

He felt tears burning behind his eyes. By his actions he had done this to her. He reached out gently and gathered her into his arms, sensing even in his grief that any sudden movements or show of emotion would frighten her.

She began to whimper as he held her, perhaps in reaction to his emotion and the tears streamed unheeded down his face. For a moment he dared to hope, but when he held her away for a moment and looked into her eyes, he found that they had not changed. Susan had blocked out everything that had happened yesterday. Her mind was blank, like a fresh page on which nothing has been written yet.

Ben Hurd picked her up. He carried her to his livery stable horse and put her up on it. He got the reins of his own horse and, holding them, mounted behind Susan. There was urgency in him now, and fear. Of Gregorio and his men. Of being captured. Of having Susan hurt again. He didn't know it, but even Gregorio wouldn't have hurt Susan in her present condition. Indians have an awe of those whose minds are different.

So Ben rode quickly back toward home, holding the horses to a trot, holding Susan in the saddle with an arm around her waist. He reached it without incident.

His wife came running when she saw them. He

lifted Susan down. Mrs. Hurd put her arm around her daughter and led her to the house. They disappeared inside. Ben realized that his wife had not noticed the change in Susan. He hoped she wouldn't notice it right away. Maybe she'd just put Susan to bed. Maybe some miracle would happen while Susan slept. Maybe she would be normal again when she awoke.

Ben Hurd was not a praying man. But he started praying now.

He put the buggy horse into the barn and gave him a feed of oats. He mounted the livery stable horse and rode him toward town. His mind was made up. He'd surrender himself to the sheriff as soon as he had returned this horse. He'd tell the sheriff everything that had happened and, whatever it was, he'd take his punishment. Only by doing so would he ever find any peace within himself again.

He reached the stable and rode the horse up the wooden ramp and through the doors. Dave Lockman met him and took the reins from him as he swung to the ground. Hurd said, "You weren't here when I got the horse. It was about dawn this morning."

"Did you find Susan, Ben?"

Hurd nodded. He didn't tell Lockman what had happened to her. Numbly he paid Lockman for the use of the horse and walked out into the street. He looked toward the courthouse and the jail, both dreading what he had to do and welcoming it as well.

A voice said, "Morning, Ben."

It was Martin Watts. He and Rufus Henshaw and

Peter Judd stood at the corner of the livery stable in the vacant lot next to it. Ben Hurd walked to them. He said, "I found Susan. All that's happened was too much for her. She's lost her mind."

The faces of the three men facing him showed no softening. Henshaw said, "So what do we do now?"

"I don't know about the rest of you, but I'm going to do what Redding did. I'm going to turn myself in."

Henshaw edged around until he was between Hurd and the street. He said, "The hell you are! By God, you got us into this! You told us that Indian had raped Susan and you got us to help you string him up! You're not going to weasel out on us now!"

"You can't stop me."

"Can't we?" Henshaw looked at Watts and at Judd, whose faces were as cold as his. With a lack of emotion that was more dangerous than anger would have been, he said, "We can kill you. Just like we're going to kill Redding and Hughie Diggs. I don't give a damn what anybody has told the sheriff, it isn't going to hold up in court against the testimony of all of us. Not if the ones accusing us are dead."

Hurd said lifelessly, "Go ahead. Kill me. You think I give a damn?"

For an instant, that surprised them. They were briefly silent and then Peter Judd said, "What about Susan and your wife? Don't you give a damn about them either?"

Hurd stared at Judd unbelievingly. He shifted his glance to Henshaw and then to Watts. The eyes of all three men were determined and cold. They would, he realized, do exactly what they were threatening.

His shoulders slumped. "All right," he said. "But Stedman will probably arrest us anyway."

"Maybe not. He knows we're not going anyplace. Not with Gregorio hanging around outside of town. And if he doesn't arrest us, we'll figure out some way of getting rid of Redding and Hughie Diggs."

The four circled the stable so that they could separate and not be seen together on the street. Before the other three left him, they warned Hurd ominously, "Just remember what we said. You talk to Stedman, and your wife and Susan won't live through the day. All we'd have to do would be to make it look like the work of Indians."

Hurd watched them go their separate ways. Like it or not, he was bound to them. They had done what he wanted the other night and now he was bound to do what they told him to do.

It seemed incredible that these men, men he had known so long and, he thought, so well, could threaten to kill his family, that they could have changed so much from the men he knew in the short span of a couple of days.

But it was equally incredible that six men, law-abiding men, could have hanged Billy Pinto for something he hadn't even done.

Desperation, fear, anger and hate changed people. He'd seen graphic evidence of that. But it seemed to be a vicious cycle that would never end.

# Chapter 14

Thorpe Stedman awoke at dawn. He always did, no matter how tired he might happen to be. He got up, rubbed his whiskered face, then went to the door leading to the cells. He opened it and looked in.

Hughie Diggs, being an early riser himself, was already awake, sitting on the edge of his cot. Curtis Redding was asleep. Stedman supposed he had lain awake most of the night. He might not have been asleep more than an hour or two.

Scratching his belly, he dumped out the old coffee grounds, rinsed the pot, and put fresh coffee on. He shook down the ashes and built up the fire in the stove. He washed, shaved in cold water, combed his hair, then stood with his back to the stove, warming himself. He intended to get Billy Pinto buried today. Max Steiner could wait a day or two. He caught himself hoping there wouldn't be anybody else, but a gloomy premonition told him the killing wasn't over yet.

When the coffee had boiled, he took a cup back to Hughie Diggs. Hughie accepted it and whispered, "How much longer you going to keep me here?"

Stedman shook his head. "No longer than I have to, Hughie." He didn't know whether he ought to arrest the other four who had participated in the hanging or not. He didn't honestly know whether Hughie would be safe outside the jail even if the four were locked up inside. They had families and they had friends and someone might get the idea that they'd be helping if they got rid of Hughie Diggs. Such an idea would have been unbelievable two days ago. Today nothing was unbelievable.

But he could decide that later in the day. Redding woke up and sat on the edge of his cot, rubbing his eyes and running his hands through his hair. Stedman said, "Sorry I woke you. Want some coffee?"

Redding nodded groggily. Stedman filled a tin cup for him, brought it back and passed it through the bars. Then he went back to the office and got a cup for himself.

The rising sun touched the clouds with red, and then with gold. The dead horse still lay in the middle of the street. Stedman went out, locked the door behind him and walked to Dallas Wagoner's house. There was smoke coming from the chimney. He went around back and knocked.

Dallas Wagoner came to the door, dressed but still unshaven. Stedman said, "I want to bury Billy Pinto today. I want to get it over with."

"All right. Just a burial?"

Stedman hesitated. He didn't know whether Billy Pinto had clung to his Indian beliefs or whether he had become a Christian somewhere along the line. He said, "We'll get Mr. Hanneck to say something at the graveside, just in case. It won't hurt anything and it will look less like we're just dumping him in the ground."

"All right. Is ten o'clock all right?"

Stedman nodded.

Silas Hanneck was the town's only minister. Stedman, not a churchgoer himself, thought Hanneck was a Baptist but he didn't know for sure. He walked back to the jail, unlocked the door, and went inside. He supposed a lot of people in Graneros were going to get upset about burying an Indian in the town cemetery alongside former residents of the town. Right at the moment, Stedman didn't give a damn who got upset. Billy Pinto had been murdered and he was going to get as decent a burial as Stedman could manage. Nobody would come, of course. But Stedman would be there, and Silas Hanneck, and Dallas Wagoner, and probably the men who had dug the grave. Stedman supposed he ought to let Hughie Diggs come too. Hughie had been Billy Pinto's only friend.

There was a knock on the door and Stedman opened it, his hand on his gun. It was Bell. He asked, "Want me to go get some meals for the prisoners?"

Stedman nodded. "Want some coffee first?"

"I'll get some at the restaurant while I'm waiting." He walked away down the street.

Stedman stood for a moment in the doorway. It was a clear, warm, September morning, with just a hint of fall in the air. Too nice a day for the kind of ugly things that were happening. He wondered briefly where Gregorio and his followers were and what they were planning for today. He wondered if the cavalry troop would leave for Graneros this morning and when they would arrive. He wondered, too, where Ben Hurd was, and where the other three were—Judd, Watts and Henshaw.

Sometime today, he thought worriedly, he'd have to talk to Serena. He'd have to tell her that her brother was one of those who had hanged Billy Pinto night before last. He hoped she'd believe him but he wasn't willing to bet on it. He also hoped he could convince her he had to be impartial. He had to treat her brother just like the others.

He knew there was a good likelihood that he was going to lose Serena over this. The idea was unbelievably depressing and he realized how much he wanted to marry her. He was tired of living alone, sleeping alone, eating in restaurants. He was tired of loneliness, of having no one to talk to, of having no one to share things with. All his life he had been alone and self-sufficient, keeping his innermost thoughts and hopes strictly to himself. He'd hoped that would change when Serena married him. Now, because her brother had joined Hurd and his friends in hanging Billy Pinto, he was probably going to lose her. The idea made him furious.

Bell came down the street, carrying trays for the prisoners. He brought them in and put them down on the desk. "Go on out and eat. I'll feed the prisoners."

Stedman nodded. Bell bolted the door after he went out. Stedman glanced toward Second Street, wondering if now would be a good time to talk to Serena or not. He decided against it. She might not be dressed. She probably wouldn't want to see him until she'd had time to fix herself up. And when he talked to her about Peter he wanted things to be exactly right.

He went down to the restaurant and ordered breakfast for himself. He ate it, gloomily preoccupied, scarcely even tasting the food. By the time he left, it was eight o'clock.

He walked to the livery stable and saddled up his horse. Dave Lockman had not yet arrived, but the stable door was never locked. Stedman rode out. He made a circle of the town, eyes on the horizons, looking for signs of Gregorio. He didn't see any but then he hadn't really expected to. At the town cemetery on the northern edge of town, two men were already working on Billy Pinto's grave. Both had brought rifles with them. They were propped up against a nearby wooden marker.

They were down about three feet and had run into gravel made up of oval-shaped rocks about an inch or so across. Stedman said, "Looks like this used to be a riverbed."

"Don't know how a riverbed could get way up here." The gravel made a rasping sound sliding off the shovel and hitting the pile at the side of the grave.

The man working in it climbed out, wiped his forehead, and the other man got down it. Stedman said, "Don't get careless. Gregorio would like nothing better than to catch you two off guard."

The man in the grave said, "If that son-of-a-bitch

comes around here, he'll get a bellyful of lead."

Stedman nodded and rode back down the slope and into Graneros Avenue. It was eight-thirty now. Still an hour and a half to go before Billy Pinto's funeral. Or rather his burial.

He rode to the church that stood at Graneros Avenue and H Street. It was white-frame, with a single spire. Next to it nestled the parsonage and across the street was the town's one-room school.

He tied his horse to the hitching post in front of the parsonage and went up the walk. Silas Hanneck had seen him coming and opened the door as he climbed the steps to the porch. "Come in, Sheriff. Come in."

Stedman shook his head. "No thanks, Preacher. I came about the funeral."

"Mr. Steiner?"

Stedman shook his head. "No, sir. The Indian's. Billy Pinto's."

"You want me at an Indian's funeral?"

"Yes, sir. He might've been a Christian. Lots of Indians are, those that live in white settlements. Anyhow, it won't do any harm to say a few words over him."

Hanneck agreed with that. "No, Sheriff. It can't do any harm."

"I told Wagoner ten o'clock. It will be a little after that when we come by here. If you'd just be watching for us . . ."

"All right, Sheriff. I'll be ready."

"Thanks, Mr. Hanneck." Stedman went back down

the walk, untied his horse, and rode down the street to the jail.

Bell let him in. Stedman said, "Go on and eat. I'll heat some water so the prisoners can wash up."

Bell went out. Stedman put a pan of water on the stove. When it was warm, he poured half of it into another pan and carried both back to the cells. He slid them under the doors, then got a piece of soap and a towel for each man. To Curtis Redding he said, "If you'll give me the key to your room, I'll go get your things. Razor and whatever else you want."

Redding gave him the key. Stedman went out, carefully locked the door, then walked to the hotel. His horse stood in front of the jail at the hitching post, idly switching flies with his tail.

He unlocked Redding's room and got the few things Redding had asked for. There was a small grip in the closet and he put them into it. He carried it down the stairs and back to the jail. Redding thanked him, got out his shaving soap and brush and began to lather his face. Stedman got him the mirror out of the office so that he could see to shave.

He looked at Hughie through the bars. "We're burying Billy Pinto in a little while. Do you want to go?"

Hughie looked scared but he nodded. Stedman asked, "Want to use my razor?"

"Yes, sir. If you don't mind."

As soon as Redding was finished with the mirror, Stedman gave it to Hughie, along with his razor, shaving soap and brush. He returned to the office. He didn't think anyone would shoot at Hughie in broad daylight, but he loaded a rifle and stood it beside the door, just in case.

Bell returned. After a while, Dallas Wagoner drove up in front of the jail with the hearse. There was a plain pine coffin in the rear.

Stedman went back and unlocked Hughie's cell. He asked Bell to look after things, then, taking the rifle, he followed Hughie out into the street. He told Hughie to climb up beside Wagoner. He mounted and fell in behind the hearse, jamming the rifle down into the saddle boot.

People stopped what they were doing to stare at the hearse as it rumbled past. They reached the parsonage and the preacher came out, dressed in black, carrying a Bible with a piece of black silk ribbon marking the place from which he meant to read. Stedman dismounted and walked with him, leading his horse. The hearse climbed the slight grade to the town cemetery.

The two gravediggers were sitting with their backs to a large granite marker near the freshly dug grave. Wagoner halted the hearse and the diggers came to help lift the coffin out. Stedman took one corner, Wagoner another, and the two gravediggers took the other end. They carried it to the grave.

Stedman removed his hat and the others followed suit. The diggers looked as though they thought this was a little silly, all this fuss over an Indian. Hanneck opened his Bible and cleared his throat.

Stedman felt it in his feet before he heard a sound. It was a vibration, a rumbling, and he knew instantly what it was. He said, "Gregorio!" and sprinted for his horse. The animal spooked away, startled by the way Stedman came at him, but Stedman managed to grab the rifle anyway.

The others were just standing there, frozen with uncertainty. Stedman roared, "Run! Get back down the hill!"

Hanneck, Wagoner, and the two diggers broke into a run down the hill. The two diggers had left their rifles behind and turned to come back for them but Stedman roared, "No time! Keep going!"

Hughie didn't seem to know what to do. Stedman pushed him in the direction the others had gone and Hughie broke into a shambling run.

Stedman turned. They came over the crest of the hill, naked to the waist, red bands of cloth tied around their heads. They started firing as soon as they saw him. Glancing back, he saw that the others were still only halfway to the nearest building that would shelter them.

He knelt behind the mound of earth that had been taken from the grave. He sighted on the horse Gregorio was riding and fired. He heard the bullet strike and saw the horse go down to his knees. Gregorio leaped clear, stopped, and fired at Stedman instantly. The bullet struck the earth mound and showered him with dirt.

With Gregorio afoot, the others, seven in all, hauled

their horses to a plunging halt. Stedman fired again, quickly, into their midst and a horse, stung by the bullet, began to buck. His rider sailed off and hit the ground on his back.

Stedman looked around. The first of those running down the hill had reached the nearest building, a shed, and had disappeared behind it. The others were close behind.

Stedman got up and sprinted for his horse, managing to put the hearse between the Indians and himself after running half a dozen steps. The spooky horse began to run before he reached him, but he managed to get the saddle horn, dropping his rifle in order to hang on.

The horse galloped down the slope, with Stedman hanging onto the saddle horn, feet sometimes dragging the ground, sometimes sailing through the air. There was a volley of shots behind but none of the bullets struck either Stedman or his horse. He reached the shed, let go, and rolled a dozen feet on the dusty ground.

The Apaches seemed uninterested in following. All were off their horses now. They opened the coffin and lifted Billy Pinto's body out. They placed it across one of their horses and one of them mounted behind it so that he could hold it in place.

Gregorio mounted with one of the others, again leaving a dying horse behind. Stedman wondered what ranch had been raided to replace the horse he'd killed the other night. He wondered what ranch would be raided to replace the horse he'd shot just now. And he wondered how many people Gregorio would kill before the cavalry captured him and took him back to the reservation where he belonged.

# Chapter 15

The Indians were gone, and the only thing remaining of their presence was a thin cloud of dust hanging in the air. Wagoner and his two diggers, Stedman, the preacher Hanneck, and Hughie Diggs came out from behind the shed and stared up the gentle slope.

The hearse stood there untouched, its two horses cropping grass. The open coffin sat beside the grave. The horse Stedman had shot from under Gregorio lay kicking on the ground. He said, "They're gone. You can go on up and get your coffin and your hearse. Looks like Billy Pinto is going to get an Indian burial."

The two diggers looked at Wagoner. "What about the grave? Do you want us to fill it in?"

Wagoner hesitated. Then he said, "No. Leave it. We can bury Max Steiner in it." He walked up the hill toward his hearse. Stedman followed. The two gravediggers put the coffin in the hearse. Wagoner got up on the seat and drove it back toward town. Stedman shot the wounded horse. He looked at the two diggers. "Want to earn an extra two dollars apiece?"

Both men nodded. Stedman said, "Get a team at the

livery barn. Tell Lockman to charge it to the county. Then drag that dead horse in the middle of Graneros Avenue over across the creek. Drag this one over the hill where it'll be out of sight."

The two men hurried away. Stedman looked at Hughie Diggs, who plainly still was scared. "It's probably better this way, Hughie. They'll give him the kind of burial he'd have wanted."

Hughie nodded. Stedman said, "Let's go back." Leading the horse, he walked back down Graneros Avenue to the jail. He took Hughie inside and locked him in his cell.

Bell had apparently heard the shots without having seen what happened at the cemetery. Stedman filled him in. Bell asked, "You think Gregorio will be satisfied now?"

Stedman shook his head. "Nope. He's enjoying this. He won't quit until the cavalry drives him back to the reservation or down into Mexico."

It was now almost eleven o'clock. Stedman asked Bell, "Mind watching the place for a few minutes more?"

Bell shook his head. Stedman left and rode to Second Street. The sun was hot on his back. The trees rustled in the breeze. A dog sat in the middle of the dusty street and scratched himself. It was a peaceful scene and the things that were happening seemed impossible.

He dismounted in front of Serena's house. His stomach felt hollow and his hands were shaking. He was scared. She knew he didn't like Peter and didn't approve of the way he managed to live without doing any work. She knew he was angered by Peter's taking money from her. She might have suspected that the reason he hadn't asked her to marry him long before this was that he didn't want Peter as a brother-in-law.

He tied his horse and went up the walk. Serena came to the door, her mouth full of pins. She mumbled at him to come in without taking them out of her mouth, then went back to pinning pieces of a dress onto a hollow dress form on a cast-iron stand.

She finished and straightened. "There." Her smile was warm. She crossed the room, put her arms around his neck, raised her face, and kissed him on the mouth. "I heard shots. What was that all about?"

"Billy Pinto's burial. Gregorio ran us off and took the body away."

Concern touched her eyes but she didn't put it into words. He liked that. She knew he was sheriff and she knew some danger went with the job and she wasn't going to nag him about changing his line of work. He said, "I've got to talk to you."

The smile faded from her mouth. "You sound grim."

"What I've got to say is grim."

"You've changed your mind?"

"No. And I'm not going to. But you might change yours when you hear what I've got to say."

She started to say something flippant, read his expression, and changed her mind. "All right. Sit down."

Stedman perched on the edge of a straight-backed chair. "It's about your brother. He was with the bunch that hanged Billy Pinto night before last."

Dismay came to her face. "Oh no!"

"Yes. Hughie Diggs saw it all. He named the six men who took part in it."

Serena's face was white, her eyes filled with dismay. It was, at first, dismay about what her brother had done. It changed into concern for Stedman and what she knew he had to do.

He said, "I've got to get back downtown. I know this is something you'll have to think about. I'll see you this afternoon."

She nodded numbly. "You have to arrest him, don't you?"

Stedman nodded. He escaped as quickly as he could. He didn't want her begging him to let Peter go. He didn't want to see her face if and when it occurred to her that he might be glad, relieved to be rid of Peter once and for all. Most of all, he didn't want her grief and dismay to trigger an argument where things might be said that both would later regret. Give her time, he thought, to think it through without any interference from him. She'd reach a decision but he hoped she wouldn't turn it into a choice between him and her brother because it didn't have to be that way.

He supposed he had better arrest the remaining four as soon as he was able to find them. Nothing was to be gained by delay. Serena had accepted the idea that he had to put her brother in jail and the longer he put it off the harder it was going to be.

Dismounting in front of the jail, he wished he weren't sheriff. He wished there was some way to avoid what he knew he had to do.

Rufus Henshaw was scared. He had spent a nearly sleepless night worrying about what was going to happen to him and to the others. Unless they did something and did it soon, they were going to be arrested and thrown in jail. They would be brought to trial and convicted on evidence given by Hughie Diggs and by Curtis Redding, whose testimony was going to be even more damaging than Hughie's could ever be. They would be sent to prison even if they weren't hanged.

As far as Henshaw could see, there was only one way out. Hughie and Redding might have told their stories to the sheriff and maybe Bell had heard them too. But if neither Hughie nor Redding was alive to testify in court, there was a chance that a jury wouldn't convict them at all. Any jury would have to be chosen from people in Graneros and Conejos County. Billy Pinto had been an Indian and everybody hated Indians. And if there was nothing to tie the four of them to the deaths of Hughie Diggs and Curtis Redding, a jury might just find them innocent.

All right so far, he thought, as the early light of dawn seeped into the window. They had a good chance of being acquitted if all they were accused of was killing an Indian. But if it was suspected they had killed Hughie Diggs and Redding to silence them, that would be something different. The jury wouldn't overlook a thing like that.

His wife had also been awake most of the night, but she was sleeping now. Carefully, Henshaw got out of bed. He gathered up his clothes and left the room, closing the door quietly behind. He dressed quickly in the hall, carried his boots downstairs, and put them on down there.

He didn't wait even for coffee, but hurried out into the cool dawn air. He went to Peter Judd's place over the saloon first, then to Martin Watts's, and last to Ben Hurd's house. He had an idea, but if they let Stedman arrest them and put them in jail, it wouldn't work.

He led the three down the bed on Conejos Creek, ironically to the makeshift shack in which Billy Pinto had lived. By the time they reached it, the sun was up. They went inside, wrinkling their noses at the smell, and stood uneasily in the middle of the room because none of them wanted to sit down.

Henshaw said, "I've got an idea but we've all got to take part in it to make it work."

The other three looked at him hopefully. Henshaw went on. "We all know that if Redding and Hughie Diggs were dead and couldn't testify in court, there'd be a chance the jury would let us go. After all, Billy Pinto was only an Indian and nobody hereabouts has much use for Indians. By the time Gregorio gets caught, they'll like Apaches even less."

Hurd was silent, plainly not liking this kind of talk. But Watts said, "If the jury suspected we had anything to do with killing them, they'd be harder on us than they would be now."

Henshaw said, "That's where my idea comes in. What if everybody thought Gregorio was the one? It would make sense. He's supposed to have broken out because Billy Pinto was related to him. He'd naturally figure that whoever Stedman had in jail was guilty, wouldn't he?"

Judd, whose face had been glum, now brightened. "It's a good idea if we can make it work."

"No reason why we can't. We'll have to stay out of sight all day so Stedman can't arrest any of us. But as soon as it's dark, we can fix ourselves up like Indians."

"What good will that do? Stedman's got the jail windows boarded up."

"I thought of that. After Gregorio's attack last night, it's not likely anybody will stand around watching if they think he's attacking again. They'll head for cover. The sheriff and that marshal will probably come out of the jail, shooting. They're not going to think about locking the door behind. A couple of us can ride on up the street and draw them away from the jail. The other two can circle around into the alley and come up on the jail from the other side. They can go in, shoot Redding and Hughie and get away before Stedman and the marshal even know what's going on."

There was a moment's silence, while the others digested the plan. Finally Judd nodded. "It ought to work. Provided the sheriff and the marshal chase the two of us up the street. But what if they come back?"

"They won't. They've both got a bellyful of Gregorio."

"But what if they do?" Judd persisted.

Henshaw said, "If they start to turn back, it will be the business of the two that went on up the street to keep them from doing it."

Both Watts and Judd seemed to like the plan. Hurd was glumly silent but nobody thought anything of it. Henshaw said, "Then let's stay right here until it's dark. Then we'll go to Ben's store. We can fix ourselves up there to look like Indians."

Judd said, "To hell with staying here. I can stay out of Stedman's sight. I know a place that I can hide."

Watts said, "Anyhow, how do we know Gregorio won't come here? We'd sure as hell be outnumbered if he did."

Henshaw shrugged. "Can all of you stay out of sight all day? Because if one or two of us get arrested, the plan won't work."

Hurd said that he could stay out of sight. The four men headed back toward town, each entering it at a different place, and from the concealment of the bed of Conejos Creek.

If any of the four had doubts about the cold-bloodedness of the plan, or regrets, it didn't show. The four were desperate, facing death, imprisonment, and the ruination of their lives, and desperate men are capable of desperate things. They had killed once and it is always easier the second time.

# Chapter 16

By the time the two prisoners had been fed, and by the time both Stedman and Bell had eaten their own midday meals, it was nearly two o'clock. Stedman left Bell in charge of the jail and he went looking for the four who had hanged Billy Pinto. Hurd was not at home, nor at his store. Judd wasn't in the saloon, nor was he in his room over it. Henshaw wasn't at his shop and he wasn't home. And Watts wasn't home and his wife didn't know where he was.

Stedman wasn't surprised. They knew he knew their names. They knew he would be looking for them. He was fairly sure they hadn't tried leaving town. They were just hiding out until they could make up their minds what to do. On the chance that he might know something, Stedman went to see Lucas Howard, the town's lawyer. Howard said he hadn't seen any of the four and Stedman believed him. Once they were in jail, though, they wouldn't be able to send for Howard quickly enough.

He rode to Serena's house before going back to the jail. What her decision would be had been worrying him ever since he'd left her earlier.

She met him at the door, no pins in her mouth this

time. Her eyes were red and she was very pale. Again Stedman perched uncomfortably on the edge of the chair.

She said, "Thank you for giving me time to think it out."

He nodded.

"It shouldn't have been a hard decision, but it was. He is my brother, for all his faults. But he has committed a serious crime. I will try to help him, but I will not let sympathy for him ruin my relationship with you."

Stedman was up off the chair in an instant. He felt like shouting. He caught her in his arms and held her. Her body shook as she wept. When she could speak, she asked, "What will happen to him?"

Stedman said, "I don't know."

"Will he be hanged?" She held her breath, waiting for him to reply.

He shook his head. "I'd say there wasn't a chance of that. Six men were involved. One is dead now, but five are left. No court is going to hang five men for killing an Indian."

"But they'll have to go to prison, won't they?"

"Yes."

"Do you know for how long?"

He shook his head. "I'd be guessing."

"Five years? Ten?"

He shook his head. "Less than that."

"He'll need a lawyer, won't he?"

"Yes." Stedman knew Serena had no money for a

lawyer. He said, "I'll stop by and talk to Howard about him."

Her face showed him her gratitude. "Can I see him?"

"I don't have him in jail. Not yet."

"Do you have the others?"

"Only Redding. Three besides your brother are hiding out. But I'll locate them."

"Is there any danger that he'll . . . ?" She did not have to finish. Stedman knew what she wanted to know. He said, "Don't worry. None of the four are likely to resist."

Soberly she said, "They hanged a man. They are afraid and probably desperate. They are all dangerous. Even Peter is dangerous."

"I'll be careful." He kissed her good-by. He left her, tears glistening in her eyes.

Glancing out across the empty plain, he thought that there was still Gregorio to be reckoned with. Not in daylight, maybe, but as soon as it got dark. He wondered if Gregorio had been raiding ranches. He doubted it. If he had, some word of it would have reached town. No, so far Gregorio seemed only interested in the town. Maybe, thought Stedman, he really had broken out because of Billy Pinto's death. Maybe he was only interested in avenging that.

He headed for the jail, tied his horse to the rail, and went inside.

Mark Rulison spent the night in an agony of

remorse. His mother hadn't spoken to him since the incident with Mr. Hurd. His nose was swollen to twice its normal size and his mouth was sore. Ben Hurd had only hit him once but he had hit with all his strength. It was a wonder Mark still had his teeth.

He refused breakfast and spent the morning in his room. Finally, in early afternoon, he knew he had to do something. He had to or go out of his mind. He couldn't stand feeling so guilty anymore. What he had done with Susan was bad enough. Running away and leaving her to face the consequences was worse. But worst of all was the knowledge that because of him Susan had been forced to lie and because she had lied a man was dead.

He got out of the house without his mother seeing him. He headed down the alley toward Susan's house. He thought if he could only talk to her. . . . He didn't know quite how, but he thought talking to her might help the way he felt.

Mrs. Hurd answered his knock on the door. He expected her to be angry and to look at him with the same disgust and contempt his mother had been showing him. But she did not. She said, "Hello, Mark." Her voice was listless and there were signs of weeping in her eyes and in the puffiness of her face.

"Can I see Susan, Mrs. Hurd?"

"Susan is not herself."

"Please, Mrs. Hurd. Just for a minute or two."

She hesitated, perhaps thinking that a visit from Mark might miraculously make Susan the way she had been before. Mrs. Hurd opened the door and Mark went in. She led the way up the stairs to Susan's room.

The door was open. Susan was sitting cross-legged on the floor. Her thumb was in her mouth. Mark said, "Hello, Susan."

She glanced up at him. Her thumb remained in her mouth. Her eyes showed no recognition. Desperately he said, "Susan? It's Mark."

She lowered her glance as if he wasn't there, as if her mother wasn't there. Mark knew suddenly that he was going to cry. He was going to cry the way he had when he was a baby and he didn't want Mrs. Hurd to see. Turning, he bolted past her and ran down the stairs.

Out into the yard he went, and out behind the stable. He put his face against the rough pine stable wall and sobbed almost hysterically. Oh God, what terrible thing had he done?

Something awful was wrong with Susan. Maybe she'd gone stark, raving mad, he thought. She hadn't known him and she hadn't even seemed to know her mother. She was sucking her thumb as if she were a baby again. And it was his fault.

He thought about his mother and the way she had been treating him. He thought about the fury and contempt in Ben Hurd's face just before Hurd smashed his fist into his mouth.

Everybody in town was going to treat him with contempt and hatred from now on. And if anybody else was killed they'd blame that on him too.

He stumbled down the alley as if he was in a daze. Because he didn't know where else to go, he went home. But he didn't go into the house. He went into the stable out behind the house where the buggy horse was kept.

He sat down, but his thoughts wouldn't let him remain still. He got up and began to pace. He had run away. In a moment of panic, he had run away. And he sensed somehow that he was going to be running all the rest of his life. From this, now. From something else later on. He was just no good. He was just plain no good for anything. Again he remembered the utter contempt on his mother's angry face. He remembered the rage in Ben Hurd's eyes.

He could run away now, he thought. He could leave Graneros any time he wanted to. Then he thought of Gregorio and his men, out there somewhere on the plain. They'd like to get their hands on him. He'd heard what Apaches did to white prisoners. By the time the Apaches got through with you, you were begging them for death.

There was a leather halter and rope hanging from a nail beside the horse's stall. He stared at it with fascination. Billy Pinto had been hanged. What better justice than that the one who had caused it also be hanged?

He took the halter and rope from the nail and stared in fascination at it. He fashioned a slipknot in the end of the rope, put it around his neck and tightened it. The rope was rough and harsh against his skin.

He was trembling violently by now, filled with terror at his own thoughts. It was a way out. It was a way to avoid the contempt and hatred he was going to get from everybody from now on.

He went to the stable door and looked toward the house. There was, in him, an almost desperate longing for his mother to see him, to know what was in his thoughts, to feel sorry for what he was going through. He also knew that unless she actually found him hanging she would think it was only a play for sympathy.

There was a wooden nail keg in one corner of the stable. Mark placed it beneath one of the rafters which had a sturdy horizontal brace. He got up on it and, standing on tiptoe, was able to buckle the halter around the brace. Letting himself down slowly from tiptoe, he felt the tension come to the rope as it tightened around his neck.

Terror engulfed him suddenly. What was he thinking about? This was crazy, thinking of killing himself. Nothing was as bad as dying, no matter what it was. If he couldn't stand the way people treated him, he could always go away. Anything was better than being dead.

He tried to loosen the slipknot around his neck, but it had been drawn too tight when he let the tension tighten it. He'd have to unbuckle the halter, he thought, and stood on tiptoe again to do just that.

He didn't know what happened. Maybe the nail keg hadn't been on a level place. Maybe he slipped.

Maybe he put his weight too close to the edge of the keg.

The nail keg was suddenly gone, rolling across the floor and out of the reach of his kicking feet. He reached up and grabbed the rope to try and take his weight off it.

But the noose had already tightened. It had already closed his windpipe so that no air could get through. He could raise himself with both hands but he couldn't loosen the noose.

The world began to whirl before his eyes. His chest ached with its hunger for air. He thrashed, and kicked, and gasped, trying to suck some life-giving air into his lungs. He failed.

His last thought before he lost consciousness was that he hadn't really intended doing this. He had wanted to be forgiven for what he had done. He had wanted his mother to discover him, standing on the keg with the rope around his neck.

That was as far as his conscious thoughts had gone. And then Mark Rulison was dead.

# Chapter 17

In midafternoon, Mrs. Rulison began to relent. A nagging feeling of guilt had been troubling her for several hours. She'd been pretty hard on Mark last night and Ben Hurd had made things worse by brutally hitting Mark in the face. The boy hadn't eaten breakfast and he hadn't showed up for dinner. Out of stubbornness, Mrs. Rulison hadn't called to him.

She went up the stairs to find his room empty. A bit concerned, she went out into the yard and to the stable, where the horse was making more noise than usual.

When she opened the stable door and saw him hanging there, turning slowly, swinging slightly back and forth, she screamed, and screamed and screamed until she was out of breath. But she didn't faint. She turned and ran frantically to the house. She snatched up a butcher knife and returned. She put the nail keg down in an upright position and climbed up on it. She cut the rope.

Throwing down the knife, she got down on her knees. There was no movement in Mark's chest. Her son was dead.

Neighbors who had heard her screams crowded in the door. Two of them helped her to the house, stunned and unable to talk coherently. Another went to bring the sheriff and Doc Ross.

Ben Hurd, hiding on the roof of his store behind the high false front, heard the commotion and saw the crowd go by, following Stedman and Doc Ross. He heard someone yell, "Mark Rulison hanged himself! He's dead!"

Feeling almost numb, Hurd sat down on the roof, putting his back to the high false front. Desperately he tried to avoid facing the truth but he could not. This was another death for which he was responsible. First

Billy Pinto. Then Steiner. Now Mark Rulison, who had done nothing that thousands of boys before him hadn't done.

Hurd felt like throwing up. The noise died out as the crowd got farther and farther away. Where was it going to stop? Not with Mark Rulison. Watts and Henshaw and Judd wanted him to help them commit two more murders as soon as it got dark. And maybe more than two, if the sheriff and that U.S. marshal, Bell, should intervene.

Anything was better, he thought numbly, than a continuation of this nightmare. Hanging. Jail. Anything was better than letting this go on and on, getting more nightmarish all the time.

Nothing could now salvage his own life. Avoiding hanging or prison wouldn't make any difference. A man had to live with himself and that was now totally impossible for him. Never, if he lived a hundred years, would he be able to forget that he had hanged an innocent man, that he had been responsible for his daughter's insanity, that he had caused a boy to hang himself. Those were burdens his conscience would bear forever. He would not permit any more to be added to the horrors he already must endure.

He had climbed up here through a skylight in the storeroom at the back of the store. Now he opened the skylight and climbed down again. Mrs. Brackett was gone, having left the store to stand in front and watch the commotion in the street.

He went out the back door. He hurried down the

alley to the jail. He went inside.

The U.S. marshal, Bell, was there. Hurd said, "I've come to surrender myself."

The marshal was standing at the window, looking out. He said, "Sit down, Mr. . . ."

"Hurd. Ben Hurd. I run the general store."

The marshal, gaunt and hard-looking, motioned to the chair. "The sheriff will want to talk to you when he gets back. Locking you up can wait."

Hurd sank into the swivel chair behind the desk. He put his face down into his hands. It was over now. He should have come to this decision yesterday, or better still, day before yesterday. But the law could handle things from here on out, and maybe he wouldn't have to feel responsible for anything else that happened.

Stedman was gone about twenty minutes. When he came back, he looked sick. He saw Hurd sitting in the chair and said with unaccustomed brutality, "Mark Rulison hanged himself. He couldn't live with what he'd done."

Hurd glanced up, face haggard. "To say that I am sorry is not enough. But I will tell you everything."

Stedman looked at Bell. "I want you to listen. You'll be needed as a witness."

Bell nodded. Stedman said, "All right, Mr. Hurd. Go ahead."

"Susan was late bringing in the cow. I went looking for her. I went a long ways and I finally heard the cow. I heard Susan's voice too. I called out to her and someone got up and ran away. I was angry. Mr.

Stedman, any father would be angry. I suppose I was so angry I frightened her. She told me it was Billy Pinto and that she had been forced."

There was a moment's silence. Then Hurd said, as if to himself, "An Indian! If it had been anybody but an Indian and a dirty one at that, I would probably have done nothing until you got back. But an Indian! And Susan was so young and she had never been touched before." He stopped doubtfully. "At least that was what I believed."

"Go on, Mr. Hurd."

"I went to my friends. I told them what had happened. We went to his shack in the bed of the creek and found him there."

"Didn't it strike you as being funny he'd sit and wait for you?"

"We weren't thinking straight. At least I was not. We dragged him out. He kept yelling at us in Apache but he didn't say anything in English. He didn't even deny what he had done."

Stedman said, "He denied it all right. But in Apache. He was likely so scared he forgot every English word he knew."

"We dragged him to that gallows across the bridge. I went to get a horse."

"And that was when Judd joined up?"

Hurd nodded. "He just came along for the excitement, I suppose."

Stedman snorted, "Excitement!" There was a moment's silence and then he asked, "Did they all know you were really going to hang him? Or did some of them think you were only trying to throw a scare in him?"

Hurd shook his head. "I don't know what they thought. I told them I wanted to hang him. Redding tried to stop us, but we wouldn't stop."

Stedman got a piece of paper out of the desk drawer. He shoved it at Hurd, along with a pencil. "Write that down. Write down the names of the men who helped you, too."

Hurd nodded dumbly. He began to write, in a small precise hand more suited to the keeping of accounts than confessing a murder. When he had finished, Stedman said, "All right, Mr. Hurd. Come on."

Hurd got up. "There is one other thing. The others will not give up. They said if I did, they would hurt my family. You have got to protect them, Sheriff."

"I'll go get them as soon as you're locked up. I think we can hold them in the courtroom next door. At least until I can find and arrest those three."

Hurd nodded. Meekly he followed Stedman back to the cells and entered one. He couldn't look at Redding or at Hughie Diggs. He lay down on the cot in his cell and turned his face to the wall.

Stedman went back to the office. He said disgustedly, "This is getting worse all the time. I feel sorry about Mark Rulison. He didn't do anything that you and I and every other man hasn't done when we were his age. The only mistake he made was running away and I expect plenty of us have done that too." He

155

sighed. "Well, I'd better go get Hurd's wife and daughter. I doubt if they'd hurt them but I'm not taking any chances. Plenty of other things have happened that I wouldn't have believed two days ago."

He went out. It was now close to four o'clock. It seemed incredible how much had happened since he rode back into town night before last.

He went straight down Graneros Avenue to A Street and turned right. There was nobody on the street at this end of town although he had seen a couple of groups at the other end, talking over the latest tragedy.

He went to the Hurd back door and knocked. He could hear no sound within the house. He knocked again. Maybe Susan and her mother were asleep, he thought. They'd probably gotten little or no sleep last night.

He opened the door, crossed the porch to the kitchen, and stepped inside. He called, "Mrs. Hurd? Anybody home?"

He got no reply. Becoming worried now, he proceeded through the house, searching the rooms downstairs before he went upstairs. The house was empty and there were no signs that any struggle had taken place. Probably they'd told Mrs. Hurd that her husband had sent for her and Susan and she'd had no reason not to believe.

He didn't really believe they would hurt either Susan or Mrs. Hurd but it was a chance he didn't dare to take. He hurried back to Graneros Avenue. As he went up the street, he stuck his head into each shop he passed, saying he wanted the man to arm himself and come to the jail as soon as possible. He went past the jail and up to the Red Dog Saloon, where he passed on the same message to the men inside.

He returned to the jail and told Bell what had happened and that he was organizing a posse to search the town. He warned Bell not to let Hurd get word that his wife and daughter had disappeared. Then he got a double-barreled shotgun from the rack, loaded it, and went out into the street.

Already half a dozen men were here. Stedman told them briefly what they had to know. "Ben Hurd has surrendered himself and so has Curtis Redding. They have named Martin Watts, Peter Judd, and Rufus Henshaw as the other three that were in on the hanging night before last. The trouble is that those three have kidnapped Mrs. Hurd and Susan and are holding them to try and frighten Hurd into keeping still. It's a stupid stunt but then none of them has done anything very smart in the last two days. I want you to spread out. I want every house and store searched. Every stable and shed, too."

The men scattered, after Stedman had assigned each group a street to search. There weren't so damn many houses in town, he thought, that they couldn't be searched in an hour at the most. The searchers would turn the three up, along with Susan and Mrs. Hurd.

In the meantime, they weren't going to hurt their hostages. They had no reason to. He reminded himself that he'd known all three for years. All three were

157

basically decent men, not criminals.

But there were six basically decent men who had hanged innocent Billy Pinto the other night. By their actions, these same basically decent men had caused a boy to hang himself.

Worriedly, he walked up Graneros Avenue, keeping pace with the searchers, shotgun ready in his hands.

# Chapter 18

According to the white men, Indians were different. Not only were they supposed to speak in unintelligible gutturals, they were supposed to think similarly. It was widely believed among whites that they had no respect for their women, and would sell them to anyone for a few drinks of "firewater." They were "savages" with no civilization and no order in their villages. They needed either to be exterminated like vermin, a view held by a surprisingly large number of whites, or "civilized," which meant subjugated, robbed of pride and sustenance, made dependent upon the doubtful bounty of their white conquerors. Little effort had ever been made to understand their civilization, which was not only highly developed, but which worked extremely well. Their relations with white people eventually boiled down to one inescapable fact. The Indians held large areas of land. The white men wanted that land and would get it no matter what they had to do.

Gregorio might not have looked it, but he was no ignorant savage by any means. He could speak both English and Spanish with a fair degree of fluency. He could write a little and he could read, accomplishments not enjoyed by at least 25 per cent of white people in the territory. More important, he understood white men and how they thought.

Billy Pinto had been the son of Gregorio's brother, who now was dead. It was true that Billy Pinto had been banished from the tribe because of the abnormality of his mind. But that didn't mean he was no longer a member of the tribe. His murder by white men, particularly the way it had been done, was Gregorio's business because Billy Pinto was a member of his family. Besides, hatred for white men was as much a part of Gregorio as the blood that ran in his veins. Billy Pinto's hanging gave him an excuse to gather followers to go on a murder spree. There was some risk, of course, that when he was finally caught he would be sent to prison in Florida. It was more likely that absolutely nothing would be done to him. White men never seemed able to agree what should be done with their red brothers who had only done what seemed to come most naturally. More often than not, their depredations were forgiven and they were returned to their homes on the reservation, the only consequence being that their stature in the tribe had been enhanced.

Still using Billy Pinto's death as an excuse to give his leaving the reservation and subsequent depredations an aura of justification, Gregorio now decided it would be pleasant to have the men who had hanged Billy Pinto. There were things that Apaches could do to men to make them wish that they were dead. One of Gregorio's favorites was the strip of rawhide bound wet around a captive's head. Stretched to its limit when tying it, the rawhide shrank as it dried in the hot midday sun. The pain lasted and lasted and was excruciating enough to drive most victims mad before death relieved them of their suffering. But maybe, he thought, with wry, white man humor, that was too barbaric a punishment. Maybe it would be better if he treated them in precisely the way Billy Pinto had been treated. Hang them, from the arm of some giant saguaro, taking care that the noose was fashioned so as to make instant death impossible, to make suffocation and strangling inevitable.

Attacks on the town of Graneros were impractical, except as a last resort. It followed, therefore, that he must find another way to get his hands on the men who had hanged Billy Pinto.

That way presented itself to him as he passed a small ranch house on his way back to town after completing the Indian burial of Billy Pinto's remains. With him were the seven followers who had left the reservation with him. The women and children were camped in a watered, shady draw thirty miles away.

From behind a low rise, they watched the ranch house. Smoke rose from the chimney. After a while a man came out, saddled a horse from the corral, and rode away. Gregorio signaled his men and they made a large circle of the house. They intercepted the man as he rode down into a deep, dry wash where they were awaiting him.

He grabbed for his gun but changed his mind when he saw the muzzle of Gregorio's carbine centered steadily on him. Gregorio said, "There is something I want you to do. If you do it well, you will not be killed." Gregorio did not mention the man's family. That would provide additional persuasion later on.

The man nodded, his face showing no surprise at Gregorio's command of English. "What do you want me to do?"

"You will go with us to Graneros. You will tell them that unless they give me the men who killed Billy Pinto, I will attack the town."

The man, whose name was Jeff Brower and who was terrified for his family, nodded. "Sure." Relief was strong in his voice. "But I don't know whether they'll do it or not."

"You had better convince them, white man. If you do not, we will return to your house. You know what we will do to your family."

Brower's face lost color. It was no use to plead. Not with Apaches. Particularly not with Gregorio, who he had recognized from pictures published in the newspapers.

They formed a column headed for Graneros. Gregorio rode in the lead. Brower was immediately behind. The others strung out behind Brower. They

161

showed no particular concern and no noticeable vigilance. But Brower knew they missed nothing on the horizons or in the land between. They missed nothing on the ground, no track of ground squirrel or road runner, not even marks made by the looping coils of the sidewinder.

He knew there was little chance he would survive what was happening to him. Not unless he was willing to forget his wife and year-old son and remain in town, which he was not. He would deliver Gregorio's message. He would return and give Gregorio the town's reply. Then Gregorio would kill him, having no further use for him. All Brower could hope for was that Gregorio wouldn't trouble to return to the ranch house and kill his wife and son.

Brower was a middle-aged man, who had spent most of his life in this territory. Most of that time he had lived alone. He had fought Apaches a couple of times, but mostly, he guessed, he had just been lucky and had survived.

Two years ago, he had met and married a Mexican woman twenty years younger than himself. He considered himself fortunate to have gotten her. He loved her as only a desperately lonely man can love someone who delivers him from his loneliness. He loved his son as he had never loved anything in his life.

He was desperate now, and scared. But not for himself. All he was thinking about was his wife and son. He had to try and outwit Gregorio if he could. But he did not intend to take any chance that would infuriate the Apache if it failed.

Gregorio took him to within sight of town. He halted his men and looked at Brower. "You will do what you have been told to do. You know what I will do if you do not."

Brower nodded. He said, "It might take some time. You know how white men are. They have to argue everything."

"I will wait until the sun goes down."

Brower rode away. He kicked his horse into a trot, wanting to go faster but not wanting to give Gregorio the idea that he was running away and might not return.

He rode into town past the gaunt and blackened gallows and the gray ashes of the old stage station, which he hadn't even known had been burned. He crossed the bridge, maintaining his steady trot until he reached the jail. Here, he looked back to see if Gregorio and his men were still visible. They were not.

He tied his horse and went into the jail. Stedman was there and so was another man, a gaunt, tall man with a U.S. marshal's badge. Brower said, "I've got a message from Gregorio. He wants the men who killed Billy Pinto, and he wants them before sundown tonight. If he don't get them, he's going to kill my wife and boy."

This was a complication Stedman didn't need. The search of the town, completed only a few minutes before, had failed to turn up any sign of the three men he was seeking, or of Hurd's wife and daughter. He didn't know whether they were hiding someplace outside of town or whether someone was hiding them. It would have been impossible to search thoroughly every attic, every cellar, every room in every house. And he wasn't sure but what there was substantial sympathy for the fugitives among the people of the town.

Gregorio's ultimatum would change all that. What sympathy might now exist would disappear. He said, "Well, I guess we'd better call a town meeting. So far I haven't been able to find the men, except for two of them that I've got in jail."

Brower knew the question was stupid but he asked it anyway. "Will you give them to Gregorio?"

Stedman shook his head. "You know I can't."

"Then what the hell do you expect me to do? He said he'd kill my family."

Stedman shook his head. "I wired for a troop of cavalry. Maybe they'll get here in time."

"And what if they don't?"

"Then maybe we can raise some volunteers to ride out to your place."

Brower knew that would be useless. They'd never get there in time. Gregorio would see them and would beat them to his house. They'd arrive to find the place in flames and his wife and young son dead.

Stedman went out. He climbed the outside stairs to the courthouse bell cupola and rang the bell. He could see people pouring into the street. Most of them, expecting Gregorio, carried guns.

He kept ringing the bell until a substantial number of citizens had come within range of his voice. Then he shouted, "We've got an ultimatum from Gregorio. I'm calling a town meeting for ten minutes from now. In the courtroom."

He went down the stairs. Brower was standing in the street in front of the jail. Stedman felt sorry for the man. He knew as well as Brower did that no force from town would ever reach his ranch house in time.

Stedman didn't really want to hold a town meeting. He could imagine the arguing and bickering that would take place, with some of the people wanting to surrender the five who had hanged Billy Pinto, the others as adamant in refusing to.

For Stedman it wasn't a negotiable issue. He had two of the men in jail and he sure as hell wasn't going to give them to any Indians. If he could prevent it, the other three weren't going to be surrendered either.

He glanced toward the west. The sun was well down in the sky. He pulled out his watch and looked at it. It was ten after five. He tried to remember what time the sun actually went down but he could not.

He could only think of one possibility. That was to figure some way of stalling Gregorio past the sundown deadline. In darkness, maybe a few men could get out of town unseen and ride to Brower's ranch.

The townspeople came in groups and singly, going silently into the courthouse. The courtroom occupied nearly all of the first floor except for a hallway and a small room that served as the judge's chambers. The people filed in and took seats. The room quickly filled.

When he thought everybody was here that was coming, Stedman went to the front of the room. "Gregorio sent a message by Mr. Brower. Either we give him the men that hanged Billy Pinto or he attacks the town. Besides that, he kills Brower's wife and boy."

A man yelled, "You mean you want us to give those men to that lousy savage?"

"That's not what I said. Gregorio gave us an ultimatum and I thought you all had a right to know about it. But we're not giving him anybody. He gave Mr. Brower until sundown. I suggest you be ready for the attack any time after that. Just remember, Gregorio only has seven men. We have a good many times that number. There is no reason for anyone to be afraid."

Except Brower, he thought. He left them to argue it out among themselves, knowing there would be some who would want to surrender the killers of Billy Pinto to the Indians. He didn't want to listen and besides, his own position could not be changed no matter what was said.

Brower was waiting for him in the street. Stedman said, "There's no use in you going back out there just to tell him we refuse. He'll kill you and after that he'll send someone to kill your family."

"Then what . . ." Brower was plainly feeling desperate.

"I'm going in there and get some men to make up a

fake party to go out and meet Gregorio. They'll make it look like they're giving up the men Gregorio wants. They'll wait until the sun's clear down and then stall all they can. While they're doing it, Gregorio isn't going to be paying attention to anything else. I figure you and me can get out of town, get to your place before he can, and bring your wife and boy back here."

The look on Brower's face was like the look of a condemned man suddenly reprieved. Stedman went back into the courthouse and told those assembled there what he had in mind. As he had expected, there was an immediate uproar. Over it, he shouted, "I want six or seven men to help me pull this off. The rest of you go home and get ready for him. Station yourself along Graneros Avenue, in upstairs windows and on roofs. When he comes through town, if he does, we can cut him to bits." He didn't tell them that in all probability he would not be here to help.

Several men came forward to volunteer. Stedman took them outside, and in Brower's presence, briefed them on the plan. Then he took Brower across to the livery stable and picked out the two fastest horses there. With them saddled and ready, he stood in the livery stable door with Brower, watching the people of the town scurrying about, getting ready for the attack.

He had apparently convinced them that he would not permit the surrender of anyone to Gregorio and they hadn't had a clear enough majority of those at the meeting to overrule his decision. Now they were doing the next best thing, preparing to defend themselves against Gregorio's attack.

# Chapter 19

The sun was just starting to dip its rim below the horizon when the men Stedman had picked to ride out and stall Gregorio gathered in the street in front of the livery. Leaving Brower and the two horses inside the stable and out of sight, Stedman went out to talk to them. He said, "Three of you hold your hands behind your backs as if they were tied. The others ride behind. He said sundown, so by God, we'll wait until the sun's clear down. If you walk your horses, it will be pretty dark before you make contact with him. Gregorio speaks English as good as I do, so he'll understand everything you say. Parley with him as long as you can, but don't let yourselves get surrounded. When you break off with him, try and kill as many of them as you can. Try to get Gregorio if possible."

The men nodded, indicating that they understood. Their horses milled around in the street while they decided which of them would be the fake prisoners. Stedman crossed the street and walked along the boardwalk to the jail. Bell was standing in the doorway, watching. Stedman said, "We haven't found Watts, Henshaw and Judd and they've still got Hurd's wife and daughter. Lock up tight as soon as I leave and don't let anybody in but me."

Bell nodded. "And if they batter down the door?"

"I don't think there's much chance of that, but if anybody tries to take the prisoners, shoot. To kill."

Bell nodded. He was a tough and veteran lawman and Stedman felt sure he'd do just that. But he didn't think there was any chance of the jail being broken into forcibly. The rest of the townspeople wouldn't permit it. They were already angry because the lawlessness of those who had hanged Billy Pinto had brought Gregorio down on the town. The three who remained free wouldn't get much sympathy from the other people of the town.

The clouds overhead faded to gray. Stedman waved at the riders milling in the street. "All right. Get out on the road where he can see you. Then travel at a walk." He watched them move out, trotting down Graneros Avenue to the bridge, then pulling their mounts back to a plodding walk.

He figured Gregorio would hang back for a while, making sure this was not some kind of white-man trap. Gregorio knew whites and knew how they thought, and he knew how unlikely it was that whites would surrender other whites, even criminals, to Indian savages.

He himself beckoned to Brower in the livery barn. Brower came out, riding one horse, leading the other. Stedman mounted and cut through the vacant lot next to the courthouse to the alley. He didn't want to be seen leaving town by any Indians Gregorio might have stationed nearby to watch. Neither did he want to be seen leaving by the town's inhabitants, at least by any more of them than necessary.

Once clear of the town, he dug heels into his horse's sides. The animal, a big, hammerheaded gray, lunged forward, running immediately with real eagerness. Behind him, Brower kept pace.

Stedman doubted if he and Brower could have been seen, either by Gregorio or by any of his men. But he didn't intend to gamble on that. If they rode for Brower's ranch as fast as their horses would go, their chances of beating the Indians there were excellent. They could have Brower's wife and son and be headed back to town before Gregorio's Indians could reach the place. It wouldn't turn into a chase as it would have in the absence of the ruse employed to make Gregorio think he was actually going to get the prisoners.

All gray faded from the sky. Except for a few stars partially obscured by a thin cloud cover, it now was dark. Brower had taken the lead, knowing the most direct route to his own place, and Stedman was following.

Brower rode with reckless abandon that betrayed his fear for the safety of his wife and son. Stedman forced himself not to consider what would happen if one of the horses put a hoof into a prairie dog hole, or stumbled, or miscalculated in the darkness the width of a jump. Leaning forward a little, weight balanced on the stirrups, he concentrated on riding and trusted the horse to see the ground.

The minutes fled past. The horses began to heat, and now and then flecks of foam blew off the gray's neck and clung to Stedman's knees. But at last, as the horses were beginning to falter and occasionally to stumble, Stedman saw the faintest of lights ahead.

It grew in size and intensity as they approached. Nearly to the house, Brower turned his head and bawled, "There's three horses in the corral. One is white. Don't take him. Bring out the other two and we'll change in case we have to try outrunning the Indians."

Stedman did not reply. When they thundered into the yard, the light suddenly went out. Brower yelled, "It's all right, Maria. It's me. Bring Bucky and come on. We're going into town."

Brower's wife hadn't known the Indians had kidnapped him but she must have known something was wrong when he did not return at the usual time. Brower leaped off his horse and ran for the house. Stedman continued to the corral. He grabbed a rope off the corral fence and went inside. The horses were galloping around and around, having caught the excitement of the two men's galloping arrival. Stedman roped one, led him to the gate, and swiftly transferred saddle and bridle from one of the livery stable animals. He went back into the corral, caught the second horse, and again changed saddle and bridle to him from the other livery stable horse. By the time he had finished, Brower and his wife had arrived. Mrs. Brower was carrying the boy, who was scared and whimpering. Brower boosted his wife up, then handed the boy to Stedman. He mounted behind his wife, kicked his horse in the sides and galloped out of the yard. Stedman yelled, "Don't go straight toward town or we're liable to run into them."

Brower veered, taking a course at right angles to the straight route toward town. He didn't spare his horse, but kept him at a steady gallop for more than fifteen minutes before he let him slow down to a trot. Looking back, Stedman saw a glow in the sky. He knew the Browers had seen it too because Mrs. Brower began to cry.

Something else for which Hurd was responsible, he thought, everything the Browers owned was gone. But at least their lives had been saved.

He wondered how things were going back in town. The fake surrender party couldn't have fooled Gregorio for very long, he thought, because Gregorio's Apaches had reached the Brower place no more than fifteen minutes after they had.

Brower slowed his horse to a fast trot. There was little chance of running into Gregorio's Indians out here, but close to town it would be different. Gregorio wouldn't have needed to send more than a couple of men to the Brower ranch. He had seven besides himself. That meant as many as six could still be near the town, perhaps surrounding it although that wasn't probable.

They reached the town by way of the knoll at its upper end where the cemetery was. Stedman saw the dead horse first, then the freshly dug grave lying open waiting for Steiner's burial tomorrow. He wondered briefly how many more graves would be needed here before this night was over with. He wondered where the hell that troop of cavalry was.

He could see a few lighted windows in town, mostly along Graneros Avenue. Otherwise the place was quiet. Maybe Gregorio was waiting for the men he had sent to Brower's place to return. He likely knew he'd need every man he had.

Brower slid off his horse in front of the hotel. He lifted down his wife, who came to Stedman and took Bucky from him. The boy had not gone to sleep, but he was drowsy and nothing further had happened to frighten him. He had been quiet most of the ride from Brower's into town.

Stedman said, "Get yourselves a room in the hotel. I'll take the horses to the livery barn." He watched them go into the hotel. Brower's legs looked a little shaky and Stedman wouldn't have been surprised if they had been shaky. Brower had lost his house and he'd damn near lost his family and his own life, too.

Stedman went past the jail and straight down to the livery. The townspeople seemed to have followed his instructions pretty well. He could see them in second-story windows and on roofs, guns in their hands. A few waved at him.

Dave Lockman was at the livery, a double-barreled shotgun in his hands. He was up in the hayloft looking out the door below the hoist. He asked, "Can you put 'em away yourself?"

"Sure. They're Brower's. I turned your two loose out at Brower's place. If they don't come back, you can bill the county for them."

Lockman didn't reply. Stedman unsaddled the two horses and put them into the corral out back. They headed for the water trough even before they rolled.

Stedman hurried up the street and crossed to the jail, glad to have been able to get back to town before Gregorio attacked.


Henshaw, Martin Watts and Peter Judd had spent the afternoon in a root cellar on the eastern edge of town. Dug out of the earth and mounded over with earth, its slanting door faced away from town and the place had therefore been overlooked.

At sundown, Henshaw ventured forth to find out what was going on in town. If the cavalry had arrived, they were going to have to flee.

He worked his way close to the center of town by staying in alleys and moving with care. In deep dusk, he saw the decoy party riding at a trot down Graneros Avenue. He saw them cross the bridge at a plodding walk. He noticed that the three men leading the group had their hands behind their backs as if they were tied.

He did not see Brower and Stedman ride out of town in the other direction. And since he had no way of knowing about Gregorio's ultimatum, delivered by Brower, he could only guess what was going on.

For a long time he stood beside a building on

Graneros Avenue studying the scene. He caught movement in the courthouse bell cupola, and finally made out the figure of a man. Briefly the man was silhouetted against the sky, gray, but light enough to outline him and the rifle in his hands.

Henshaw studied the roofs of the other buildings along the darkened street. He saw several more men on the opposite side and assumed men were also stationed on roofs and in second-story windows on this side of the street.

Quite obviously, the town was ready for Gregorio and expected him to attack. What the purpose was of the group that had ridden out just after sundown, he had no idea, but he assumed it might have been a group trying to negotiate with the Indian.

But if negotiations failed, and they would, the town didn't intend to be taken unawares.

Henshaw carefully withdrew from his vantage point. Scowling, he returned to the root cellar where the others were. They had a lamp going and the place smelled of smoke and of kerosene.

Swiftly he told them what was taking place in town. Mrs. Hurd sat in a corner on a pile of sprouting potatoes, watching them with frightened eyes. Susan's expression still was blank. She seemed neither to know, or care, what was going on, although her face was streaked with tears from a session of crying earlier in the day when she had wanted to leave and had been refused.

Henshaw said, "There's no use even considering our

175

other plan, the way things stand now. I say we'd better get out of here, go on downtown, and see if we can't figure out something new."

"What about them?" asked Judd.

"We can leave 'em here, with the lamp. It'll burn for a long time. The door opens out so we can jam a pole against it to keep them from opening it."

The plan seemed agreeable to the other two. Mrs. Hurd seemed glad to see them leave and did not protest their leaving her. Outside, they found a pole and wedged it against the door, effectively jamming it tightly shut.

All three knew that raiding the town was out of the question now. If they were dressed as Indians, they would be mistaken for Indians by the men stationed along Graneros Avenue waiting for Gregorio to ride into town. They'd probably all be killed. Certainly they'd have no chance of getting into the jail to kill the prisoners. That plan had depended on taking the town by surprise.

Judd asked sourly, "Got any more bright ideas?"

Henshaw didn't much like the sarcasm but he said, "As a matter of fact I do. We hide in the alley behind the jail. When Gregorio attacks, and judging from all the preparations he must be going to, we just move in and carry out our original plan. A couple get between the sheriff and the marshal and the jail. The other one goes in and does the dirty work."

Judd asked, "And who's the one who goes in and does the dirty work?"

Henshaw knew Judd wouldn't do it. And he didn't think Martin Watts had the cold-blooded nerve the job was going to take. He said, "That's my job. Is that what you wanted me to say?"

Judd grunted in the darkness. Henshaw said, "Then let's get in position right away. We've got no way of knowing when this attack is coming off."

# Chapter 20

Thorpe Stedman knew he'd just as well forget about the cavalry. If they hadn't arrived by now, they weren't coming at all tonight. He'd never known a cavalry unit to move in darkness, except, of course, during the war. The troop, if it was on the way at all, was probably bivouacked at least a dozen miles from town. So much for the help you could expect from the government, he thought bitterly. But he was really not surprised. The last time Geronimo had gone on a rampage it had taken five thousand U.S. troops months to capture him and even then they would have failed except for forty or fifty Apache Scouts.

So the town of Graneros was on its own. He didn't know exactly how many men were occupying vantage points along Graneros Avenue. Probably less than twenty-five were able-bodied and old enough to use a gun.

Still, two to one were good odds in any fight and the townsmen had an additional advantage in that they were hidden. Gregorio and his followers would be exposed.

At nine, he went out for a walk along Graneros Avenue to make sure everyone was alert and to make sure the best vantage points were occupied.

The hotel lobby was jammed with women and children. When their men had left to man posts along Graneros Avenue, the wives and children, afraid to stay alone, had come downtown to the safety of the hotel. Glancing up, Stedman saw men in three of the darkened upstairs windows of the place.

He thought of Serena Van Vleet and wondered where she was. He stuck his head into the hotel lobby and asked the nearest woman, "Is Mrs. Van Vleet here?"

"I haven't seen her, Sheriff. Maybe she's still at home."

Stedman nodded. Serena's house was directly west of the hotel on Second Street, so he cut through the vacant lot beside the hotel and went straight to it.

A light was burning in the parlor. He climbed the two steps to the porch and through the window saw her still working. He knocked.

She came to the door, apparently completely unaware that an Indian attack was imminent. Stedman said, "Blow out the lamp and come to the hotel. Gregorio may attack the town."

She didn't question him. She hurried to the lamp, blew it out, picked up a shawl and came to the door. He hurried her across the street, through two weed-grown vacant lots and around to the front door of the hotel. He said, "Stay under cover. There may be a lot of bullets flying around if he comes up the main street the way he did last time."

She nodded, her glance clinging to his face for a long moment before she turned and went inside. He headed back toward the jail, warmed by the memory of the way she had looked at him.

Something troubled him, something vague, and he tried to decide what it was. He finally decided it was doubt. Gregorio was not a fool. He not only spoke good English but he probably understood the way a white man's mind worked better than any Apache alive.

Gregorio would know an ambush was waiting for him along Graneros Avenue. It was possible, of course, that he was arrogant enough and reckless enough to ride into it if only to show his extreme contempt for it.

It was more likely that he would make a different kind of attack. But what kind? And how could Stedman defend against it, if he hadn't the faintest idea what form it was going to take?

He knocked on the jail door. Bell called out asking who it was and Stedman identified himself. The door opened. Bell said, "It's getting late."

Stedman grinned. "I wish that story about Indians never fighting at night was true."

"You think he'll be fool enough to ride up Graneros Avenue?"

179

Stedman shook his head. "Not unless he just wanted to show his contempt for the white man. Huh uh. I think he's smarter than that."

"Then what will he do?"

"I guess we wait and see."

"He might bring his men in from both sides, sneaking them in one at a time. Apaches like to fight that way."

"I know it. But how the hell do you defend against an attack like that? If I got a group together and sent them out to patrol the town the Indians would slaughter them."

He didn't mention it to Bell because he didn't even want to put it into words, but Stedman was worried about something else. Gregorio understood the workings of a white man's mind. And understanding it, he would know that the thing a white man feared most, especially in a town, was fire.

How better to draw the white men from their hidden vantage points than to set a series of fires on the edges of the town? And how the hell would he combat such a tactic, if and when Gregorio adopted it?

The answer to that was scary. There wasn't any way. If he let the townsmen go fight the fires Gregorio would pick them off one by one. If he tried to prevent the townspeople from fighting the fires, the whole town would probably be consumed. Particularly tonight, with a brisk breeze blowing out of the west.

He looked at Bell. He could see that the marshal was thinking the same thing he was. He said, "I can't just sit here and let it happen. You can bet your life that if we've thought of it, Gregorio has too. It could happen any time and once it starts there'll be no stopping it."

"What else can you do but wait?"

"I only know of one thing. Go out there and try to find him before he finds me. If I could kill Gregorio, the rest of them might figure it's bad medicine and hightail it back to the reservation. After all, Billy Pinto wasn't *their* relative."

"I'll go with you." Bell got up and started toward his gun, leaning against the wall.

"Huh uh. Somebody's got to stay here. Those three would still like to kill our prisoners, remember?"

"You won't have much chance alone."

"The prisoners wouldn't have any chance if we both left this place."

Bell nodded reluctantly. Stedman got a double-barreled, ten-gauge shotgun from the rack. He got a big handful of shells loaded with buckshot from the drawer of the desk. He loaded the gun and put the extra shells in his pocket. The shotgun's range was short, but he wasn't going to get any long shots anyway.

As he went out the door, he said, "Keep it locked. If they try to batter it down, put a shotgun charge through the middle of it."

Bell nodded. There was no sign either of worry or fear in his face. Thank God, thought Stedman, for Bell's presence here. Without him he wouldn't have had a chance of saving his prisoners.

He cut around the side of the jail, along the passageway between the courthouse and the jail. Weeds and trash rustled beneath his feet. Just before he reached the end of the narrow passageway, he heard a sound in the alley ahead of him, but he couldn't identify it and when he reached the alley it was empty. At least so far as he could see in the faint light coming from the stars.

The wind sighed through the bell cupola behind him. He headed west because that was the direction from which the wind was coming. If Gregorio set fires, it would be on the western side of town so that the flames would be blown toward the rest of the town instead of away from it.

He was almost certain by now, in his own mind, that fire was the weapon Gregorio was going to use. Had he intended an open attack up Graneros Avenue it was likely he'd have made it long before this. Besides, he had used fire to destroy Brower's place and the old stage depot and blacken the gallows, and it wasn't likely he'd overlook it now when it could be of such great advantage to him.

He crossed Second Street, glancing to right and left, looking for horses, for skulking shapes, seeing nothing but glad Serena was safe at the hotel.

Fire told him where Gregorio was. Set in dry weeds beyond the edge of town, it swept toward a line of stables, fences, outbuildings, and shacks that formed the western edge of town. Set in half a dozen places at once, it made a series of blazes at least two blocks long. Near each fire as it caught, Stedman glimpsed an Indian and nearby, in most cases, the Indian's horse.

How long, before the fire would reach the line of dry wooden buildings, he wondered. How long before they caught? And how long before the blaze grew enough to spread to the houses beyond?

Half a dozen Indians, spread out and setting fires in the weeds. Gregorio sure as hell wasn't one of them, he thought. Gregorio was somewhere nearby, another man with him, because he'd had seven followers. But where? Damn it, where? In minutes the whole sky was going to be ablaze. This end of town would be damn near as light as day.

Carrying the shotgun across his chest, he broke into a run. Suddenly, from behind a shed directly in front of him, two horsemen appeared.

Their horses were frightened by the smoke and were being difficult to control. Otherwise, Stedman wouldn't have seen them before they saw him. He roared, wondering what kind of stupid sense of chivalry required that he warn the two before killing them. "Gregorio! Throw down your gun!!"

Neither Apache showed any intention of complying with the demand. Both turned toward him, both trying to bring their rifles to bear. Only the nervous antics of their horses prevented them from doing so, even momentarily.

Stedman raised the shotgun to eye level and fired. The range was such that the buckshot charge spread exactly enough to spray both horses and both men.

The horse Gregorio was riding reared, lost his balance and went over backward, coming down in the alley dust with a crash. The other horse went to his knees, stayed that way an instant, then folded over on one side.

Stedman raced half a dozen steps closer, cocked the other hammer and raised the gun to eye level a second time. Gregorio had dropped from the saddle of his rearing horse an instant before the animal went over backward and was now nowhere to be seen. Stedman didn't know whether he had been hit or not. The other Apache, wounded, had slid from his horse when the animal went to his knees. He was down behind the horse's carcass now, rifle steadied on the horse. Even as Stedman squeezed the trigger of the shotgun, the muzzle of the Indian's gun billowed smoke. A blow like the kick of a mule took Stedman's leg out from under him and dumped him in the dirt. The charge from his gun, at shorter range than before, nearly took off the Indian's head.

Stedman looked at his leg unbelievingly. The Indian's bullet had torn a hole in his thigh from which the blood freely flowed. He was down, and hurt, and he hadn't gotten Gregorio, and in a minute this place was going to be swarming with Indians.

Using his empty gun as a crutch, not daring to take the time to reload it, he got painfully to his feet. There had been a moment when the leg was numb but now it felt like a red hot iron was searing it. Face contorted, as angry as he was hurt, Stedman limped toward the dark side of the nearest shed.

He saw the movement out of the corner of his eye, swift movement like that which might have been made by a charging, leaping animal. He knew what it was before he turned his head. Gregorio, who must have lost his gun when his horse reared and fell backward, but who must surely have a knife or weapon of some kind.

Stedman, half a yard from the wall of the crumbling shed, slammed himself toward it with a violent push against the gun he was using as a crutch. Gregorio struck him at almost the same instant.

The slashing knife cut a deep gash across the muscles of Stedman's back, which instantly felt warm with the rush of blood. He had no time to think that now, here, in this dusty alley he was going to die. He had no time to think at all. All he could do was react with the instinct that is as old as the species itself, the instinct to preserve one's life.

His shoulder struck the shed, and gave him leverage and support. He raised the shotgun, holding barrel in one hand, stock in the other, and faced the second slashing attack from Gregorio, whose face was contorted, whose eyes blazed red in the reflected firelight.

The Apache, and the knife, came raging in and Stedman raised the shotgun to fend them off. Knife blade slid along the metal barrel of the gun, bit deep into the walnut stock, and cut Stedman's hand, with most of its force already gone.

But Stedman knew defense was not going to be

enough. Gregorio had six more followers out there in the weeds, who were even now approaching at a run having been alerted by the three gunshots. Raising the gun, even before the knife had been withdrawn, Stedman pushed it forward and then brought it down savagely, with all the force of which he was capable.

It struck Gregorio's forearm with numbing force and the bloody knife dropped into the dust at Stedman's feet. For the barest fraction of a second Gregorio stood frozen there, eyes on the knife, debating whether or not to dive for it.

He could have simply stepped back and waited for his men. But that was not the nature of the man. He was one in a thousand, as wild and savage as this wild and savage land that had been wrested from his people so brutally. He was an animal, wearing the form of a man. He hesitated only for the barest instant, then dived forward for the knife. This was his fight, this was his enemy.

Stedman, bloody back braced against the shed, bleeding leg supporting only part of his weight, slid one hand down until both hands held the shotgun by the barrel. As Gregorio dived forward for the knife, he raised it clublike high above his head.

Gregorio's hand closed on the handle of the knife. He started to roll, then changed his mind and came forward, raising as he did. The knife was held with the sharp edge up, and would have slit Stedman open from crotch to breastbone in half a second more.

But the gun was coming down. With all the strength

and force of which he was capable, Stedman brought it crashing down.

The stock struck Gregorio squarely on the top of the head, shattering as it did, but first making a noise like a cleaver striking a butcher's block. Gregorio went down, his face driven into the dust at Stedman's feet, his head dented visibly from the blow.

Gregorio was dead, but Stedman was hurt and unarmed. He whirled to face the approaching Indians.

Over on Graneros Avenue, Stedman heard a shotgun blast, muffled as if by enclosing walls. He heard shouting, shouting that drew closer with every passing moment.

The six remaining Apaches stood less than fifty feet away, their eyes on the still body of Gregorio. Would they kill him, Stedman wondered. Or would they conclude that their medicine had turned bad and retreat?

It was only a few seconds but it seemed like a lifetime to him. He let his breath sigh slowly out as the six turned and trotted away toward their horses, standing beyond the line of blazing weeds and grass.

And now the townspeople arrived. The bell in the courthouse began to ring. Using what was left of the shotgun as a cane, Stedman hobbled toward the jail. Behind him the townspeople scattered to put out the grass fires, licking at the first buildings at the edge of town.

The door of the jail was open, its lock blasted away by a shotgun charge. Stedman stepped through the door, dropping the ruined shotgun and drawing his revolver as he did. His leg was weak and he was losing blood but he couldn't quit yet.

Bell sat at the desk in the swivel chair. Blood from a head wound was running down his face into his eyes, which had a stunned, uncomprehending look. The door leading to the cells gaped open.

Bell's shotgun lay on the floor at his feet. Nearly falling as he stooped, forced to steady himself on the desk, Stedman scooped it up. He jammed his revolver back into its holster and checked the shotgun's loads.

All he had to do was wait, here, with the shotgun trained on the door that led to the cells. The three who had hanged Billy Pinto would come through. But he knew that by the time they did, Hughie Diggs and Hurd would both be dead and probably Redding too.

He took a step toward the door, the shotgun poked out in front of him, both hammers cocked, his finger on one of the triggers.

He heard the clang of a cell door as it was opened. He heard a wordless bawl of anger at the same time he heard a woman's cry from the doorway leading to the street.

He hesitated an instant. He turned his head and saw Serena standing there. With her thus exposed, he knew he couldn't wait. If any one of the three came through the door and fired at him, she would be directly in the line of fire.

Ignoring both his leg and her pleas, he charged toward the door leading to the cells. His leg, weak and numb, let him down and he nearly fell. Staggering, he slammed against the left side of the doorway with a crash.

But he had support and the shotgun was level in his hands. Ahead of him, in the corridor between the two rows of cells, he saw Judd and Martin Watts. Henshaw was inside Ben Hurd's cell. A gun was in Henshaw's hands and it was pointed straight at Hurd. Knowing Hurd was only an instant from being killed, Stedman roared, "Henshaw!"

Henshaw whirled. Judd and Martin Watts dived along the corridor, frantically trying to get out of the line of fire. Out of the corner of his eye, Stedman could see Redding standing white-faced and frozen in the center of his cell. Hughie Diggs cowered in a corner, trying to make himself as small a target as possible.

Stedman raised his gun but he couldn't fire. Not with Hurd standing just beyond. He opened his mouth to yell at Hurd to get out of the line of fire, knowing even as he did that he was too late. Henshaw's shotgun muzzle looked like the mouth of a cannon and Stedman knew that any instant it would belch smoke and death.

Too late, he regretted the hesitation that had kept him from firing. His own life was at stake and he shouldn't have hesitated about the risk to Hurd.

In that split second, Hurd hit Henshaw from behind. The shotgun was thrown off line and the left barrel belched smoke and shot. The charge caught Judd, crouched on the floor in the corridor.

Henshaw pulled free of Hurd, whirled and swung the gun savagely. It caught Hurd on the temple, crushing his skull, dropping him to the floor with neither a movement nor a sound. Henshaw tried to come around, again trying to bring the remaining barrel of the gun to bear on Stedman.

Stedman fired. The charge took Henshaw in the chest and drove him back. Knowing how deadly Henshaw's shotgun was, even in the hands of a dying man, Stedman dropped to the floor. Henshaw's shotgun roared, its buck-shot rattling on the bars of the cells and cutting the air where he had stood only an instant before. Then Henshaw crumpled, to lie partly across the body of Hurd, also dead.

Watts, the only one remaining, raised his hands and yelled, "For God's sake, don't shoot me! I give up!" and Stedman gestured toward the open cell door with the barrel of his gun. Watts stumbled in, skirted the two bodies, and sat down, trembling, on the cot. Stedman staggered along the corridor, slammed the cell door, and turned the key.

He turned and glanced toward the office. Serena stood in the doorway, her horrified glance on her brother's body. Stedman knelt and felt Judd's neck for a pulse. There was none.

He had no idea how much she had seen or whether she believed he had killed her brother or not. It didn't matter, though. Her eyes were shocked and stunned and horrified but when she raised her glance and looked at him he knew her chief concern was for him.

Relief that he was alive made tears well up in her eyes and spill across her cheeks, made her mouth tremble almost uncontrollably. He dropped the shotgun, hobbled along the corridor, and took her in his arms.

He held her trembling body for a long time, conscious of his blood leaking away but not wanting to let her go. Bell appeared behind her, unsteady but now in possession of his faculties. He said, "You'd better sit down and let me do something about that leg."

Serena immediately pulled away from him. Between the two of them, they got Stedman to his office chair. Serena began, with trembling hands, to rip up, for bandages, the sheet that had been on the cot. As she worked, Bell asked, "Did you drive off those Indians all by yourself?"

Stedman, now feeling pain in both his leg and back, grinned weakly. "That's what I'll claim at election time. The truth is, though, that when I got Gregorio the others figured their medicine had gone bad. They lit out for home."

Serena, kneeling and trying to stem the flow of blood from the wound in Stedman's leg, said impatiently, "Both of you, be still. And send somebody for that tooth-pulling horse doctor. I need some help."

Bell went to the door. Stedman watched Serena's hands. He hurt and he was weak from loss of blood. But he had felt worse. He sure as hell had felt a lot worse than he did right now.

**Center Point Publishing**
600 Brooks Road ● PO Box 1
Thorndike ME 04986-0001 USA

(207) 568-3717

US & Canada:
1 800 929-9108